Once Upon A River

by

Dee Farrell

Illustrated by

Haley Jula

Once Upon a River
ISBN:9780976626817
Cover Image: Flying Eagle Publications and Haley Jula
The Raisin River, Monroe, MI.

Illustrations: Haley Jula

Christian Historical Fiction

Printed in the USA

"...For You [Jesus] were slain, And have redeemed us to God by Your blood Out of every tribe and tongue and people and nation."

Revelation 5:9

Once Upon A River

Adelle Chaboillier

The full moon illuminated the river like a shimmering silver ribbon. It cast dappled shadows along the sloping banks, and the forest stood dark and silent on either side. At the bend where the river turned inland, a pile of rocks littered the shore and stretched lazily to midstream. Water droplets trickled and splashed among them, spilling into currents that had flowed in the same direction for generations.

Adelle Chaboillier sat on a smooth rock at the water's edge. Upriver a moose splashed in the shallows, and she watched as he lifted his head and shook it side to side, the moonlight gleaming on the spread of his wet antlers. A breath of air, small as a whisper, rustled through the trees. Its subtlety was deceiving, for the seasons were passing as they had always passed, time upon time, memory upon memory.

A fallen leaf twirled downward from the forest shadows, catching in the swirling pool at her feet. She reached for it in the cool water. In the light of day the leathery oval leaf would be a bright lemon yellow. But here in the darkness, its beauty was unknown. How so the things of this world are not what they seem, she thought. Here in the permeating darkness of a fallen world vessels made to shine cannot. But where the Light is accepted, the eyes of the heart are open to see Truth and revelation dawns.

Adelle tossed the leaf out into the flowing liquid silver. She had faith the sun would rise in the morning, and its light would make known to the world the glorious creation the leaf was meant to be. She knew, because she had come to believe it once upon a river.

Old Northwest
1746-1747

A Changing Wind

There was a sense of urgency in the air. Adelle Chaboillier felt it pulsing through the hardwood beams of the little trading post. Autumn in New France always roused the trappers from their summer lairs. They needed winter supplies for the fur season, and the last few days her father had done a steady business. A good omen he had said.

Adelle had come here with her father to the remote shores of the Rivière aux Raisias to establish a winter post according to terms agreed upon at Fort Pontchartrain. This arrangement limited competition with other traders clustered near the fort. It also satisfied the Indians living near the river as well, since they didn't have to travel so far for supplies. But the snows would begin soon, and all of nature would slow down, even an Englishman.

The English indeed. Adelle frowned at the thought of them. They scanned the riches of New France with a jealous eye and a greedy heart. She emptied the contents of the last canoe pack and laid a hefty bag of blankets on the counter. Well, Pierre would do his part in keeping them from filling the west. She smiled slowly and without intending to. She just couldn't help herself. Pierre was a soldier at Fort St. Joseph, but he would be returning soon with the militia headed for Pontchartrain. Her heart filled at the thought of seeing him again.

The sturdy wooden door creaked its now familiar welcome as it opened, and a stream of sunlight spread across the plank floor. Three Indians entered as silently as wolves. Their heads were cleanly shaved except for the crown where a shock of porcupine hair stood straight up adorned with a feather at the back. Hurons.

"Is Monsieur Chaboillier here?" one of the Hurons asked her in perfect French.

Adelle looked at him again, this time more closely. He spoke French with only a hint of the Huron accent, and he was slightly shorter than his companions. Although his skin was tanned and his cheekbones fairly high, he lacked the full lips and hooked nose characteristic of the Huron people. The other Hurons ran their brown fingers over the laces of the tailed snowshoes hanging on the wall. They seemed to approve of the workmanship.

"My father will be with you in a moment," she replied in her native French. She motioned toward the loft. "He is discussing business."

He nodded, eyeing the tools and trinketcases newly piled on the floor. He was about forty she guessed. Black dye was smeared around his eyes in a concoction of grease, probably bear as this was a common base for the Indian people to use in such things. It surrounded the entire socket from his brows to his temples, and a line was drawn across the bridge of his nose to connect it all together. Fine rays, also black, radiated from above his brows along his forehead and from the outside corner of his eye, over his cheekbones to his earlobe. From there the thin lines continued in shorter lengths downward to his jaw and halfway to his chin.

These were not idle decorations, Adelle knew, for each Indian, each tribe, had their distinctive marks and identity. Like their clothing, it revealed their personality and accomplishments. With growing interest she observed the meticulousness of his appearance. More lines were drawn across his thickly muscled upper arms like the claw swipe of a cat. These marks were repeated on his bare thighs between his breech cloth and leggings. His scalplock, the long hair left at the back that was a warrior's pride, was braided and adorned with two eagle feathers and a strip of red cloth. It was a sign of great bravery and courage, an honor not easily won.

He waited patiently, the whites of his eyes shining brightly against the black paint as he carefully took in the details of the little post. His gun rested lightly in the crook of his elbow, and a thin piece of dark hair hung from the barrel.

Adelle shuddered. It was possible the hair came from a trade buffalo tail or mane, but more likely it came from an enemy. Adelle had never seen him before, but then she wasn't familiar with the trappers in this part of New France. She did know that this man's attire distinguished him as a powerful warrior. His presence was commanding and his countenance dignified. He was clearly the leader of the trio.

Adelle stooped to pick up a stack of shirts and bundles of twine. Thus began the arduous task of piling all the goods on the shelves behind the counter. Before she had finished a stool scraped across the floor of the loft. The sound of voices grew louder as Adelle's father and Jean Michel LeClere, a trader from Pontchartrain, descended the stairs. He had brought supplies with him for her father to trade.

Monsieur Chaboillier moved slowly, his health not what it used to be. "Monsieur DuPree," he addressed the stranger.

Adelle jerked her head up sharply. Surely this man was not French! Her father must be mistaken.

Nevertheless, this man her father identified as DuPree nodded in reply as the old man took his place behind the counter, his eyes narrowing when he saw LeClere, deepening the lines at his temples.

"Reynard what a surprise to see you!" Chaboillier continued, grasping the man's hand warmly. Adelle wondered if he noticed DuPree's obvious displeasure with their guest.

LeClere greeted DuPree also, smiling broadly, but his eyes were cold balls of lead. Reynard DuPree said nothing in return. His friends laid a bale of beaver and musquash pelts on the counter. Chaboillier caressed the furs. With seasons of experience behind him, he determined their worth.

"These are fine, Reynard, but the prices. You know they are down." He spoke softly with regret, for the French traders were restricted by license fees and controlled markets. Also, an overabundance of pelts had saturated the market, driving the prices down.

Chaboillier named his price, and DuPree related the information to his friends. Adelle understood some Huron, even though she was more familiar with the Algonquian dialects of the Pouteaouatami and Outawae with whom her father traded. Huron was Iroquoian. But one didn't have to speak the language to understand they were unhappy with the amount. Their disgruntled faces told all.

LeClere chuckled as he pulled on his deerskin coat. "You should explain to your friends that is a generous offer, Reynard. It is hard times. Perhaps they need to be reminded they must accept what is fair for their ally, New France. It is the duty of friendship after all."

Reynard DuPree's icy stare should have frozen LeClere to the spot, Adelle thought. Still, he said nothing.

"Oh, I almost forgot," LeClere told Chaboillier. "I brought a letter for you." He reached into his pack. "I will be back this way before winter sets in. I told Maillet I would meet him at the mouth of the Kankakee."

"Very well," Chaboillier replied, taking the letter. "Give him my regards. Also, bring back about 300 plank nails if you can."

With a nod, LeClere left. The chilly late afternoon breeze swept in as he closed the door. Goose bumps climbed up Adelle's arms, making her shiver.

"And now where were we?" Chaboillier handed Adelle the letter, his full attention given to DuPree.

"Let them have whatever supplies they want," Reynard offered. "I will be responsible for the difference. On credit of course."

Since most business was on credit anyway, the agreement was made. Reynard would bring bales of pelts in the spring to pay off his debts.

Adelle quickly scanned the letter as her father piled the requested supplies on the counter. "It is from Ducharme, Papa. He says he is doing well." Adelle looked up for her father's reaction. Instead, she met Reynard's piercing black eyes widened in surprise. She smothered a smile. It was unusual for a girl in New France to be able to read, but the Jesuits had taught her.

Reynard DuPree slid the last of the supplies across the counter and gathered them in his arms. He turned to go, his sudden betrayal of emotion expertly covered by an air of superior indifference. The other Hurons were already loading their canoe.

"I'll see you in the spring then!" Chaboillier called after him.

From the doorway, Adelle watched them paddle out of sight down the river. "Papa, how do you know Monsieur DuPree? Have I met him before?"

Chaboillier limped outside and sat on a large upturned piece of firewood still needing to be split. "Ah-h." He rubbed his knees. "The cold, she is coming."

Adelle followed him. "Papa?" she questioned again.

"Reynard DuPree is mètis," he answered. "The mongrel race they so dread in Quebec, yes?" His tone dripped with scorn, for the leadership there frowned upon wasting French blood lines. "His father was French; his mother was Huron. Wendat is their word as you know."

Adelle nodded her understanding. Huron was a derogatory name. Even though the tribal names were spoken by the traders as best as they could understand them, there were also nicknames and shortened names bestowed that were purely French in perspective. But Papa insisted on using the Indians' own words as a means of respect and expected her to know them.

"He used to trade north of Missilimakinak with his father when he was just a boy. His father was my partner in the old days. Good man, but got himself killed by these woods." Chaboillier shook his head.

Adelle waited for him to go on.

"When I brought trade goods to Pontchartrain, I heard they were missing and went looking for them. I found Reynard; he was happy to see me, I guess. I brought him back with me to Pontchartrain to his mother's people. After that I saw him only briefly.

"The last time was in Pontchartrain three years ago. He was in trouble there." Chaboillier chuckled. "He is fiercely loyal to the Indians, and that puts him at odds with the French vanities, yes?"

Adelle sat cross-legged on the ground. "What kind of trouble?"

"Well," Chaboillier answered with a smile and rubbed his graying beard. "He had caught some trader cheating an Indian woman and was trying to make a public example of him."

"Who was the trader?"

"I don't know," Chaboillier said quickly. "I didn't stay to watch. Was not my business, and I didn't care to look on another man's misfortune. 'Twas not new for a trader to cheat an Indian anyway, eh?"

Adelle squinted into the setting sun. "I do not think he likes LeClere."

The old man laughed softly. "DuPree's kind do not have much use for a talker like LeClere. DuPree is a strange man I think, but he has always been honest with me. And there is something to be said of an honest man, no?"

Adelle hugged her knees to her chest. "Papa, there is something I want to talk to you about. I've been thinking of it all day."

"All day?" Chaboillier repeated in amazement.

Adelle took a deep breath. She knew this would not be easy. "I want to meet Pierre in Pontchartrain."

"I cannot leave –"

"I know that, Papa," Adelle interrupted him. "I could go myself."

"Pontchartrain is too far."

"You have raised me to take care of myself, have you not? You know I can make it to Pontchartrain."

"Yes, you are capable. But you forget you are a woman!"

"A woman who can take care of herself as well as any Anishinabekwe."

"Ha! You have never travelled alone. It is different. And think of what might happen–"

"Nothing is going to happen," Adelle assured him.

"Ah, spoken with the confidence of youth. No. My answer is no; you will not go to Pontchartrain alone."

"But Pierre–"

"Pierre will wait," Chaboillier interrupted. "He will wait if he is worth waiting for." He seemed doubtful.

Defeated, Adelle walked to the river's edge. She did not want him to see her tears. Papa did not like Pierre. She knew that, but he wasn't being fair.

Papa was quiet at supper. Adelle wondered if he were angry with her. She cleaned and put away the supper bowls then went outside to gather an armload of firewood. A half moon shone its watchful gaze over the apricot dusk. Chaboillier sat in his beached canoe hunched over his fishing net like an old bear, engrossed in his task and oblivious to the world. She squatted next to the wood pile, digging for big pieces at the bottom.

"Tomorrow you will go to the Pouteaouatami village and ask for Joseph." Chaboillier's deep voice drifted to her on the evening breeze. But there was something in the quiet that followed that made her turn around. He sat with his hands folded, staring into the bottom of the canoe. He seemed to be unsure of his next words.

"If Joseph is wintering near Pontchartrain–" He hesitated. "If Joseph is wintering there, you may go with his family. Ask him if he will take you to the fort."

Adelle stood up, firewood piled high in her arms. "Thank you, Papa." It was all she dare say for she wanted to scream with joy, and Papa would not like that. He considered such things foolishness. Instead, she smiled so hard it hurt.

Chaboillier watched her. How well she guarded her emotion; it was almost amusing. If only... If only Pierre Antoine would be worthy of her. But then, maybe no man would be worthy in his eyes. He shrugged his shoulders. It was time, he knew. She was a woman now, older than most for marrying. He would have to let her go. He had tried his best to raise her, but he was a man, and Adelle had matured with a roughness about her. Perhaps this would become distasteful to an educated man like Antoine.

He dropped the net into the bottom of his canoe. The forest seemed quieter than usual; odd, he thought. Chaboillier knew his life grew shorter. Adelle would need someone, someone who would love her as much as he. "Please protect her, God," he whispered to the river. "She is yours."

The water lapped at his moccasins as he stood for one more minute at the river's edge. Was he making the right decision? A primrose glow shaded into the blue sky above the trees as the sun sank behind them. He believed he was, but that didn't make him feel better. Perhaps she was ready to go out on her own, but he hadn't prepared his heart to see her go. A wedge of geese passed overhead, the whisper of their wings the only sound. A lone honk haunted the late October chill long after they had disappeared.

Pierre Antoine trudged along, too tired to join the conversation of his companions. The setting sun warmed his back as they made their way eastward. These cursed Fox Indians were more of a bother than anyone expected, he thought. It was a time of relative peace, and his orders were to open the way west for French expansion. Instead, he and his superiors were turned back by the Fox who fought viciously to maintain their land. And what would it matter if he and his companions had won? New France had only a handful of soldiers to defend and hold a country bigger than France itself.

It was of no use, Pierre despaired. Had he not seen the English when he was in Quebec? They fought with an eye to what could be gained while his king gave no thought to what could be lost. A poor Frenchman had himself, his furs and the governor. In that order, Pierre thought bitterly. Well, not anymore. Not for Pierre Antoine.

Soon he would be joining the ranks of the independent coureur de bois, the rover of the wood. These men were not confined by any authority in the trading of their goods. They sold to the highest bidder, whoever that may be. And rightly so, Pierre thought. The French government deemed this trade illegal, but a man did not need a license to make his living, Pierre reasoned. As soon as he could, he was heading to the Guyahauga Creek country where trade was good and the high British bid close by. For all he lacked, there was one area he excelled in: his slyness. Pierre smiled a slow spreading smile. He already knew what he wanted to do. Now it was just executing his plan.

"Are you lost in the thought of a soft, sweet smelling mademoiselle?" One of his companions elbowed his ribs.

Pierre laughed in reply. But it was a hollow empty laugh.

Reynard DuPree stared into his fire. A rabbit hung over the flames browning nicely. The Wendats, a bit too loudly for his taste, contented themselves with emptying a bottle of brandy. He ignored their revelry tonight, though he had been known for his own carousing in the past. Tonight his thoughts sobered him.

He was on his way back to the Wendat village south of Pontchartrain, and the news he would bring them would please the elders. Still, he was troubled. But the answer to this trouble was right here in his hand. It could be his for the taking. So why did he hesitate? Out of respect for Chaboillier, he already knew. He would go to Chaboillier then, and talk it over. If Chaboillier agreed, all would be well. If he did not, so be it. He had been given the chance, and his fate was his own.

He felt the tug of his French heritage like a nagging pain, but the love of the People was the only love he knew now. And now he was willing to sacrifice his only tie to his French past. His jaw tightened as he thought of the consequences of such a sacrifice. So be it. He would do it for the good of the People.

He cut a slice of meat from the spit, and the fire hissed as the juices dripped into the hot coals below. A baleful spirit descended over him, but he willed it away with the hardness that had shaped him. It was settled then. No matter how he might wish it otherwise, he would not turn back.

The morning dawned crisp and clear. A light frost covered the meadow. Adelle cleaned the breakfast bowls quickly and grabbed her pack. She did not want to give Papa time to think over his decision of last night. He had seemed distracted this morning, and Adelle feared it had to do with her leaving.

"I am ready, Papa," Adelle called to him as she crossed the small clearing. She dropped her pack into her canoe.

Chaboillier rounded the corner of the little post carrying his axe. He swung it neatly into an old stump as he passed. "So I see. You do not waste time?" He almost smiled. "Life is dull here with your papa?"

Adelle turned to face him. "Papa," she scolded.

He pulled his knife from the sheath on his belt. "Take this with you."

"But I have my own knife," Adelle objected.

"Do you talk back to me, Adelle? I said take it with you. I want you to have it."

Sliding her own knife into the side of her legging, Adelle took his knife and slipped it into the sheath fastened to her belt. A sudden gust of wind picked up the fallen leaves at her feet and sent them rustling across the path. Wisps of hair tore loose from her long braid.

"Adelle, you had the courage to tell me what you desired; now I must have the courage to tell you what weighs in my heart." Chaboillier looked out across the river. "Your mother would be pleased with you." He smiled at her. "You are as beautiful as she, yes?"

Adelle had never known her mother. The woman had given birth to four children before Adelle, and all had died shortly after. It was ironic then, that after finally birthing a healthy child, she died.

Chaboillier smoothed the stray hairs from her cheek with his blunt calloused fingers. "But listen to me this one thing. Do not spend yourself for something that has no worth, Adelle. That is life's biggest tragedy. It is the makings of regret."

Adelle gazed into the eyes that had cared for her, had loved her for eighteen years. "How will I know what is worthy, Papa?"

He looked down at her, and his face held an expression of earnestness that she had not seen before. "Something is worthy if it is true and it is lasting, yes? And that you will only know by the Voice in your heart."

Adelle gave him one last hug. "I will remember, Papa," she told him. She climbed into her canoe and picked up the paddle by its throat.

Chaboillier pushed the canoe into the current and waved to her from shore. "Tell Joseph I said hello!" he called across the water.

Adelle looked back over her shoulder and waved. Seeing Papa standing on the shore, she suddenly felt a wave of doubt. A hot tear fell on Adelle's cheek, but she turned and sliced her paddle blade cleanly through the rippling current.

The forest glowed in the distance, sparkling saffron and russet. The river mirrored the splendor above it, and faded green lily pads floated in the cool shadows. A vulture glided in the air overhead. It turned with a slight tip of its wings, and the sun flashed across the velvety feathers of its back.

Adelle delighted in being on the river. The water rushed together in the murky current, drawing her, holding her. It calmed, it encouraged and it inspired. Papa had taught her what he knew of God, and the Jesuits in St. Joseph tutored her also, but it was times like this that she felt the closest, felt the certainty of God. She thanked Him often for His gifts. Today was a gift, she thought, a promise unfolding.

The Pouteaouatami village was half a day's journey downriver. They often travelled to the mouth of the river to gather rice, and some of them wintered near Pontchartrain. Chief Francois Joseph was friendly with her father. Papa respected him– trusted him. Surely he would not object to taking her with his family to Pontchartrain.

The sun warmed her face as she finally neared the village. Adelle's heart beat faster as she jumped from her canoe and pulled it to shore.

Chaboillier pulled his snareline and lifted the musquash he had caught for his dinner. Adelle would be nearing Joseph's village by now, he thought, squinting into the noon sky. He stood and carried the musquash to the cabin. Something didn't feel right. He searched the tree line at the edge of the meadow.

A crow's rash call erupted from the top of the trees. The flock swirled in a flurry of black feathers and harsh cries. Chaboillier dropped the musquash, slapping his hand to his empty knife sheath. Desperately he ran for his axe still buried in the tree stump. But it was too late.

A falling leaf rustled softly in its descent and nestled on the moist forest floor. A hawk's cry pierced the air as the bird leaped into flight from its perch high overhead. Adelle watched its grey underside and brown patterned wings pass above her just as a cloud covered the sun. It was as if the hawk had pulled a blanket over the canopy of trees, declaring judgment on those below, she thought. Adelle pushed her way through a tangle of red dogwood. She had a bad feeling in the pit of her stomach.

The village was just ahead, but the only sounds Adelle could hear were the sounds she made. No smell of smoke was in the air. She felt weak with anxiety until at last she reached the clearing.

The village was empty. Surely she had already guessed it would be so, she thought, but the reality was no less disheartening. Adelle staggered to the black circle in the middle of the lodges and stirred the burnt remains of the cooking fire. No red glow appeared when she blew into the ashes. She slumped to the ground, tears burning her eyes. She was too late; they had left, perhaps yesterday. Maybe there was time to catch up to them.

"No," she argued with herself. Her canoe was not sturdy enough for the lake which would be rough this time of year. Not even Papa travelled far from the shore. It was not uncommon for a canoe to split apart or go down. That would be a foolish risk she didn't have to take. She had no choice. She would have to go back and wait for spring as Papa had said.

She got up, wiping her tears on her sleeve. The promise of the day had turned to bitter disappointment. She made her way back to the canoe and shoved it into the water. She jumped in, angrily slapping the water with her paddle. Her sobs echoed against the trees.

By the time the afternoon light had waned into the rosy glow of evening, Adelle rounded the last bend and the post came into view. It spread peacefully along the grassy shore of the river where Papa had built it set back almost to the tree-line to avoid the spring flooding. Adelle frowned, searching to see if he were outside. Her head ached from crying and squinting against the sun on the water.

"Papa!" she called as she pulled her canoe to shore, but he did not answer. There were footprints in the wet sand, Adelle noticed, but they were not Papa's. Visitors had come. He was probably tired and resting. Adelle reached for her pack and headed for the cabin. Maybe it was better that she came back to stay with him after all. He was getting older, though it was hard to believe sometimes. In spring, maybe she could persuade him to stay in Pontchartrain with her. She smiled. That would take some doing.

She glanced at the old stump as she passed it. Papa's axe was still sunk in its flesh. But something made her turn again to the axe. She stopped, dropping her pack on the ground beside it. The ground was scuffed and the grass torn. She followed the trail of disheveled earth. It led to the cabin.

"Papa," she breathed. Adelle squatted down, her heart racing, her hand on Papa's knife. If someone else was in the cabin they had probably heard her call out. She crept close to the ground as she had been taught, coming ever closer to the window opening at the side of the cabin. She flattened herself against the wall and drew Papa's knife from its sheath.

She heard nothing. Holding her breath, she peered inside. No one. She pulled herself up tall as she kicked the door open. She ran inside, diving and rolling to one side as well as any Indian brave, but no one challenged her. Goods were strewn across the floor, the pack of brandy emptied, the flour barrels spilled open. Then she saw him.

Chaboillier lay on the floor behind the counter in his own blood, a knife wound in his chest.

"Papa!" Adelle screamed. She rushed to kneel beside him. His vacant stare told her what she didn't want to know. Papa was dead. Murdered.

The shock held back the tears for the moment. She looked around the room again. A raiding party must have attacked, she reasoned, and Papa had tried to fight them off. They were probably drunk, she thought bitterly. They could come back.

"Oh Papa, what must I do?" she asked aloud. Adelle caressed his graying hair and the tears began to swell in her eyes. She blinked, her tears falling on his face. "I cannot leave you like this," she whispered.

Chaboillier was a thickly set man, and Adelle struggled with his weight as she dragged him outside. She dug a shallow grave for him and covered it with rocks.

"I am sorry, Papa," Adelle apologized. "But I must hurry." She squatted next to his grave, placing her hand upon the pile of cool rocks. "Thank you for him, God," she prayed.

She rose slowly, not willing to leave him. "Oh Papa," she said through her tears. "If I had only been here with you." You would be dead too, wisdom told her.

She took one last look at the crude grave, tears still streaming down her cheeks. "Good bye, Papa. Good bye." She silenced the cries rising in her throat and shakily took a deep breath. Cautiously she walked back to the cabin, gathered what supplies she could and tossed them into Papa's canoe. In the dark, she paddled silently downriver.

She made her way slowly for she was not accustomed to travelling the river in the dark. True, the current lumbered along as if it headed uphill, she thought wryly, but the rocks and fallen limbs were still there to navigate around. LeClere was almost two day's journey to the west, and Joseph was now at least three day's journey to the east. She was alone with a raiding party about and perhaps a trapper or two, but none she would trust with her safety.

At the first rays of light she pulled her canoe into the shallows and hid it. She crawled into a thicket, concealing herself as best she could. Sleep came gradually, but it was fitful, broken with waves of overwhelming emotions of fear and grief, and by late afternoon she was anxious to put more of the river behind her.

She wiped her swollen eyes on her deerskin sleeve. "I must eat to keep my strength," she reminded herself, sternly. "Papa is gone." The tears almost started again, but she blinked them away. "I must think of myself now. I have to get to Fort Pontchartrain."

She sighed shakily. Reaching into her pack, she pulled out pemmican and dried corn. If Papa had insisted she stay with him, she would be dead or captured which could be worse than dead. She realized also that Papa, without ever knowing, had saved her life. Papa may not have known, but surely God did. He was the One who had saved her life. He had changed Papa's mind. But why not save Papa?

The question brought back the tears, and the dried meat grated against her throat as she tried to swallow. "Oh God, why my Papa?" But there was no answer.

She leaned wearily against the rotted log in her hideaway. Wiping her nose on her other sleeve, she closed her eyes and waited for the night to come.

A half moon peeked through a veil of low lying clouds. It was both a blessing and a bother, Adelle thought as she picked her way silently to the water's edge. It was a blessing that she could see where she was going, but it also made her easier to see. Adelle found her canoe and quietly pulled back the gnarled willow branches she had used to cover it. A twig snapped behind her.

Adelle froze, her heart thumping in her chest. Vainly she searched the shadows beside her as far as she could see, barely turning her head. She moved her hand slowly and deliberately to rest on the handle of Papa's knife still in its sheath on her belt. Painfully, fearfully, she waited for another sound. One minute. Two. Three. But none came. She let her breath out slowly between clenched teeth and grabbed the gunwale of her canoe. Probably only a deer, she thought. A cluster of dark clouds floated over the moon. Suddenly, she was grabbed from behind.

"No!" Adelle yelled, squirming to free herself. Her arms were firmly pinned to her sides, but she kicked with all her might and tried to bite the arms that held her. The smell of brandy was strong as her attacker's hot breath roared in her ear. He pulled her away from the canoe, and someone else took hold of her legs. She writhed and twisted fighting as best she could in hoped they would drop her. But they had the advantage of surprise and strength. They carried her, wrestling and thrashing, into the forest.

Adelle strained to get a look at the liqueur-stinking pair as the passing clouds revealed the moon once again. The light was still dim in the shadows of the forest, but she could not mistake the silhouette that held her legs: tall, muscular, with a center shock of hair that stood straight up. It was the Hurons, those bristly pigs!

They carried her into a clearing and dropped her on the ground near a crackling fire. Reynard DuPree emerged from the darkness and into the circle of light.

"So, you have come to me, yes?" he said in French. He smiled down at her, his teeth white against his dark skin, the fire creating dancing shadows on his face.

The Plan Unfolds

"Murderer!" Adelle spit at him.

Reynard laughed. "I have no intention of murdering you, mademoiselle."

"You murdered my father!" Adelle kicked the Huron attempting to tie her ankles together.

"Your father is dead?" Reynard and the Hurons exchanged glances. "I did not kill him," he said.

"Do not try to deceive me," Adelle declared menacingly, even though she had lost her battle with the Hurons and now sat bound hand and foot.

"Mademoiselle, I am many things, but I am not a liar. Now tell me what happened." Reynard waited.

The firelight deepened the lines at his eyes. Adelle searched his face. He could be telling the truth, she decided. Her father had said he was honest. Still... "Maybe it wasn't you," she declared. "Maybe it was your drunken friends!" She jerked her head toward the Hurons. "Cases of brandy were stolen. They were angry were they not? Perhaps they were angry enough to want revenge." Adelle met his fierce glare. "Perhaps they killed him for you."

Reynard squatted next to her. "There is no time for your useless prattle," he said. "Now tell me what happened, or you will wish you had."

Adelle hesitated. What was it like to die? The image of Papa's bloody body filled her mind.

"Now!" Reynard shouted. His eyes were furious with impatience, and his nostrils flared. The black grease on his face glistened in the yellow light.

She wanted to cry, but she was able to keep her voice steady as she told him what she knew. He stood and related her story to the other two men. They spoke together for some time in Huron, their speech rushed and anxious. Her knowledge of the language being limited, she only understood tiny scraps of useless words. One word, however, Yondotin, she recognized. It was their name for the fort. And another was a word like patience, as in waiting for a harvest. One thing she was sure of: they seemed worried.

Reynard looked down at her. "We must go," he said. He drew his knife and held it up. The blade gleamed in the firelight. Adelle swallowed hard.

Roughly he pulled her long hair to one side. "It was probably a raiding party that attacked your father. Maybe Miamis. Whoever they are, they may still be near. If a Frenchman comes, he may know you are missing. As long as no one sees you, they will think you were kidnapped by the raiding party." He cropped her hair off just above her shoulders.

"If they see you with me, or when LeClere hears of this, then I will be the suspicious one, no? Augh! This complicates things."

He threw her hair into the fire, untied the rope at her ankles and jerked her to her feet. Adelle grew nauseous at the smell of her burning hair.

"We must disguise you as a Wendat woman for now. You will be safer," he told her.

"But why–"

Reynard paid no attention to her. He gave directions to the Hurons who quickly doused the fire and collected their things. Reynard guided her down to the river in front of him. Their canoes were hidden as well and very near hers. Just her luck, Adelle thought. But why would they go to the trouble of hiding their canoes? She didn't get a chance to ask. She was tossed into a canoe with Reynard. One of the Hurons took hers.

"Why do you want me?" Adelle questioned Reynard as he pushed off. "Why must I go with you? "

"In time," Reynard said. His jaw was set, and the muscles in his cheek tightened.

She leaned to one side. It would be so easy to upset the canoe and swim to the other shore. Reynard glanced at her. But it would be just as easy for them to overtake her. Indeed, she was no match against three men with her hands tied. Escape was only an idle dream. Adelle fought back the tears as her shoulders shook in agonizing sobs.

"Enough!" Reynard whispered hoarsely. "Shut up and sit there." He raised the canoe paddle as if he were going to hit her.

Adelle glared at him. "I will kill you the first chance I get," she promised, gravely.

Reynard chuckled, and the whites of his eyes flashed in the darkness. "That is why you are tied. Now shut up."

A Huron village lay to the north, but not as far as Pontchartrain. Adelle guessed that is where they were taking her. They followed the shore of the lake making good time. The men were skilled canoeists, more so than even voyageurs, and they must have known this country well to be able to travel the lake at night, Adelle thought. Reynard hid the canoes at dawn, and they rested during the day. Later that evening they turned into the Rivière aux Hurons, and soon they had reached their destination.

Huron children ran to greet them as Reynard and his friends dragged the canoes from the river. Two women came also, probably the men's wives, Adelle guessed. Reynard helped her from the canoe.

"Now what?" Adelle sneered. "Am I some Huron's slave?"

Reynard stood in front of her, his darkened eyes drawn into thin slits. "It will go well with you if you remain silent. Keep your ignorant French slang to yourself. When you are with me, you will call The People by their name, Wendat. It means people who live on a peninsula." He took her by the arm and pulled her towards the village.

Adelle saw a man standing in the distance. He seemed to be waiting for them like one who had practiced watching. Their arrival was of some importance, or was it just curiosity over the odd sight she must be? Reynard's breath quickened as they drew nearer, and she felt his grip tighten on her arm, not so much out of fierceness, she decided, but out of excitement.

She could see the old man easily now. His coat and leggings were elaborately embroidered with red vines and flowers. A circular, feathered cap crowned his head, and a headband, also embroidered, came to a point in the middle of his forehead. Adelle knew enough about the tribes in the area to recognize that the clothes and manner identified him as the chief.

"Ayesta," Reynard greeted him.

He was taller than Reynard, and must have been a powerful warrior in his time, for he was still a formidable presence.

"I return with good news of our brothers in Orontondi's village," Reynard continued. "They are well and send you their greetings."

The old man nodded. "It is good for our people to be one again. Come, you must tell me of your journey."

Reynard put his hand on the old man's shoulder. "There are things to tell that trouble my spirit, Ayesta. But there is a hope for this trouble that stands here with me."

"What hope must be bound like the feet of a deer? Come we will speak of these things together with the elders."

The old man led them into the village past a young bear in a cage. A kind of cheering chant went up all around them as the braves followed. "Ho! Ho! Ho! Ho!"

Adelle felt the stares as she was escorted to the biggest longhouse that stood inside the village circle. She had never been this close to a longhouse before. It was a huge, elongated dome-like structure with poles running the length and width supporting a criss-crossed layer of smaller poles lashed together over a bark covering. The interior of the longhouse was dim, lit only by the fires that stretched along a middle aisle. The smoke escaped through holes in the roof like a chimney, but a lot less efficient. Living compartments for each family were sectioned off by deerskin curtains, and it looked as if two families shared a fire. Adelle counted twelve fires so twenty-four families occupied this one longhouse. Sheets of bark covered the floor. They stopped, and the old man seated himself next to his fire. He motioned to Reynard.

"Sit," Reynard told her in French, and she sat down.

More men and women soon gathered with them. An elaborate clay pipe was passed from man to man. Again and again it made its rounds among the Indians until finally the old man spoke.

"My son, Mighty Fox, has returned from the great chief Orontondi's village," he began. "His lips bring the words from the mouth of our brother. Let us hear the wisdom he has brought us."

All eyes turned to Reynard. "The great chief, Orontondi sends his greetings to Old Coyote, to his brothers," Reynard said. "He asks you to remember the day of his leaving. How the French angered him like the red-winged blackbird angers the sparrow, taking from him what is not his to take. So it is with the French, they take from us our furs and give us next to nothing in return. He determined to make their enemy, the English, his friend. He asks you to remember his love for his people on that day. How he led them to Saundustee."

Reynard paused, and the elders' gaze was full upon him. "Orontondi has allowed the Pennsylvanian to build a trading post in his village."

The elders looked quickly one to another. This must be a bit of a surprise, Adelle thought.

"He wants to tell his brothers that he has found happiness for his people. He has given his permission to the English to trade with the people of his land, the Miamis and the Shawnee. "

An elder seated across from Reynard held up his hand. "This news that you bring is good to my ears. It brings the sun's light into my eyes. That is my thought on the subject."

"A-au!" the other elders declared in agreement and the pipe was passed again.

Reynard held up a string of tiny shell beads attached to a wooden handle with notches carved in it. "Orontondi invites you to council, Old Coyote," he said. "To speak with the chiefs of the Wendat. To talk over these things that have happened with the French and the future of the Wendat." The pipe was passed again.

"My son," Old Coyote said after the pipe had been smoked for some time. "You have told me that along with the words you bring us, you carry a heaviness in your spirit. Tell us of this sorrow here among the council."

"While I was with Orontondi, I traded for the people with other traders. Some were French on their way to the post on the Maumee." Reynard gripped his bare leg nervously. "On my way here I had a dream a Frenchman killed a turtle that held two feathers. These were the feathers of Orontondi. My people, I fear our great chief is in danger from these men."

Old Coyote listened gravely. "Mighty Fox has been given much okie and he is the dreamer of dreams for his people," he said. "We must consult together what this means for the People."

The Plan Unfolds

The elders were quiet. The old chief gestured to a young brave sitting near him. Adelle understood that the brave was to remove her from the council. So she was not surprised when he approached her, pulled her to her feet and guided her outside.

It was dusk now, and children ran in front of Adelle, busy in their games. They stopped for a look at her, but with flashes of orange sunlight on their gleaming black hair, they quickly turned and went on their way. Huron women were bent over their cooking platforms which were poles lashed together like a table frame with more poles resting horizontally on top to form a two-tiered cooking surface. Kettles and fish were placed on these shelves, and the whole apparatus was placed over the fire. Some of the women carried babies in cradle-boards which were strapped to their backs and decorated with tinkling strings of shells and bright paintings.

Adelle followed her escort along the winding village paths until he brought her to an old woman sitting outside a longhouse. The young man gave her directions and left. Adelle understood what was said, and knew the woman was supposed to watch her.

The woman untied her hands. "If you run away, they will kill you," she said in French. "Eat." The woman handed her a bowl of steaming venison stew and motioned for her to enter her living quarters.

"Merci," Adelle said and took the bowl. She had forgotten how hungry she was. The last thing she ate was her pemmican, and that was almost two days ago.

The interior of this longhouse was the same design as the other, Adelle observed. The woman motioned for her to sit down near her fire. She sat on a platform covered with furs. Her shoulder length hair was greased flat to her head and hung in a braid tied with snakeskin. She had sharp features, and Adelle thought she must have been very beautiful in her youth.

"What is your name?" Adelle asked in between bites of the stringy, tough meat.

"Marie." The woman gave her French name.

"Marie, what are the elders talking about?"

"I do not know," Marie answered.

Adelle watched her. She was lying. "Of course you do," Adelle scoffed. "I know that Hur-, um, Wendat women are very important in tribal affairs."

But Marie sat on her bunk as still as a stone. Adelle had to content herself with silence as she watched Marie embroider a piece of black deerskin with moosehair thread. Soon the flames of Marie's fire hypnotized her, and the heat relaxed her weary body. She felt strange, like she was in a dream.

A dog barked nearby, and Adelle thrust open her eyes. She must have dozed off, she thought. The fire was low, and Marie still sat across from her, but the deerskin was folded in her lap. Adelle cleared her throat and stretched.

"He comes," Marie announced and motioned for Adelle to follow her outside.

Darkness had begun to set, but the fires cast an orange glow among the longhouses. Reynard strode across the clearing towards them. "You will sleep in this lodge tonight," he informed her sullenly. He stooped to pick up his canoe pack on the ground.

Adelle gritted her teeth at the sight of him, sudden anger shooting through her like a flash of lightening.

Marie disappeared into the longhouse, and Adelle and Reynard were alone. She saw her chance. She drew Papa's knife from her belt and lunged at him. Some unseen sense betrayed her though, for he turned and caught her just in time. But not before she had sliced his hand.

"You still have your knife, yes?" He mocked her French. "My mistake." He took the knife from her with his bloody hand and forced her to the ground. "And I will take this one too." He pulled the other knife from her legging. "If you really want to be sly, keep your knife to the inside of your leg so its outline cannot be seen." He smiled at her.

"I hate you!" she screamed. Adelle beat his head with her fists. "You are a dog!"

Reynard struggled to re-tie her hands as she wrestled him with all her might. She was surprised by the ferocity with which she fought, as if her very being was engaged in the battle for its freedom, for her life the way she had known it before Papa– before Papa–

"You foolish woman!" Reynard yelled. It was some time before he regained control, and a circle of laughing braves gathered around the tussling pair.

With a vicious, final yank on the rope around her ankles, Reynard sat back on his heels, smiling up at his friends. Briefly examining his wounded hand and stained, torn leggings, he rubbed his jaw where Adelle had placed a well-timed kick. The young brave from the council laughed and said something Adelle did not understand, something about eiachia. Reynard and the others joined in his laughter. Then Reynard pulled her to her feet, the tightness of the cords making her flinch in pain. The men turned to go as Reynard roughly carried her inside the lodge and dropped her on the fur covered mat Marie had prepared for her.

He bent low over her so his mouth almost touched her ear. "If you were anyone else, you would be dead," he whispered. His warm breath sent shivers down her spine.

She closed her eyes, and when she opened them, he was gone. Sleep was hard to come by as the cords cut into her flesh, and she throbbed with pain. In the morning, she was exhausted.

Marie bent over her, gently tapping her cheek. "Sit up, and I will untie you."

Adelle sat up. She felt as if she might faint. The air was so thick with smoke she couldn't breathe, and she felt nauseous. Marie massaged her wrists, and as the dizziness left, Adelle could see they were the only ones in the lodge. "Thank you," she said weakly.

Marie rubbed her shoulders. "You need to eat," she answered motherly. She brought her a pile of corn cakes, and Adelle ate them slowly.

Adelle leaned against the pole wall of the longhouse. "You are very kind to me," she said as she finished the last cake.

Marie straightened the mat and furs. "Lie down and sleep. Reynard will be back soon. You need to rest."

Adelle did not argue. She felt like she could sleep all day. "Marie?" Adelle touched her arm as she turned to go. "Why am I here?"

Marie hesitated, looking thoughtful. "Sleep, Adelle," was all she would say.

Adelle was confident she knew more. "Who is Reynard DuPree?" she tried again.

Marie brushed Adelle's hand away. "My son," she replied and was gone.

Adelle lay back down. Kind Marie was his mother? It was hard to picture a man like Reynard having family. It seemed more reasonable that he just emerged from the ground, from the hell he was destined to return to. She imagined Reynard standing amid yellow, flickering flames. The fire burned hot, and he grimaced in pain. "I did not kill your father," he whispered. Then Adelle fell asleep.

The Plan Unfolds

Near the shore of Lac de Michigami, a young officer stood at attention as his commander examined the ragged group of soldiers.

"Only one man missing, sir," the officer reported.

"Surprising," the commander replied gravely. "These wretched savages are cunning, entirely fierce in their determination. Regroup men," he addressed his small company of soldiers. "They may be planning another ambush. We will be reaching Pouteaouatami territory soon. The man missing– what was his name, officer?"

"Pierre Antoine, sir."

"Most unfortunate," the commander said. "Most unfortunate, indeed."

Adelle awoke with a start as Marie tapped her cheek. "Quickly," she urged Adelle. "I must tie you."

Groggily, Adelle sat up, blinking her eyes open. Marie tied her hands, but thankfully not as tight, Adelle thought. Minutes after Marie left, Reynard entered the lodge. Adelle admired her craftiness.

Reynard sat down across from her. "Good morning," he greeted her. "I hope you are ready to be cooperative today. Perhaps a long night has stilled some of your fire?"

Adelle smothered the defiant smile that so desperately wanted to express itself.

"Well then," he continued, accepting her silence as submission. "I wish to speak with you, and if you promise not to try and kill me again," he smiled in a brief pause. "I will untie you." He waited for an answer.

Adelle studied him. He was so confident. "I cannot say that I would not like to see you dead." She paused just as dramatically. "But I will not be the one to kill you. No. I am going to pray you die a long slo-ow death."

Reynard laughed. "I think I will take you at your word then." He moved behind her to free her hands. He smelled not unpleasantly of tobacco smoke and sunflower oil. "Let's get you something to eat," he said. He pulled the deerskin hanging at the door to one side and waited for her.

Her wrists and ankles smarted from the rope burns, and she flexed her fingers gingerly as if they still pained her so he would not be suspicious. The last thing she wanted was to get Marie in trouble.

Outside the afternoon sky was bright blue and feathered with white, wispy clouds. Gratefully, Adelle inhaled the clean air. It took a minute for her vision to adjust to the daylight after the darkness of the lodge. Reynard handed her a bowl of fish with wild onions, and Adelle gladly took it from him, settling herself down on the ground, fully intent on devouring the fresh food. His hand was wrapped in a bandage, and a bruise had formed at the side of his face where she had kicked him. It was too large to be hidden by the black markings, she observed, though that fact didn't seem to bother him. He sat calmly beside her watching the activities of the busy village spread out in the clearing. But Adelle sensed his thoughts were elsewhere.

What did he want from her? She wondered. Could she believe he did not kill Papa? She set the empty bowl down in front of her. Believe, believe, it did not matter what she believed, she decided in disgust. What was the truth? This she must know. "Did you kill my father?" she demanded, alert for the slightest hint of guilt.

Reynard met her questioning glare evenly, and though the fullness of his gaze was upon her, and the nearness of his powerful presence sent chills down the back of her neck, there was no deception in his expression, not a flicker of emotion in his eyes.

"Chaboillier was my friend." He emphasized his words with a shake of his fist. "I did not kill him."

He spoke almost kindly, but Adelle knew by his tone that he meant the matter to be final. There seemed to be other things on his mind.

"You said you wanted to speak to me," she said. "So speak." She was disappointed he seemed so sincere. Perhaps he was not Papa's murderer; she did so want to cling to his guilt, but she also held the notion he could not be above such an act if for a purpose that suited him. Indeed, one did not gain a red cloth and two feathers as was in his possession for such measly crimes as stealing brandy.

Reynard stood up. "Come," he said, and Adelle brushed herself off and followed him. He led her to a deserted path that wound its way through the forest.

Adelle looked about her. "This is far enough," she said.

He took her by the arm and pulled her forward. "You do not decide." He didn't stop until they reached a place where the backwater of the river filled a small depression, creating a quiet pond. He leaned against a dead maple and peered across the smooth water.

Adelle saw again the hard lines in Reynard's face and remembered Papa's friendship with his father. She wondered if any part of his French father remained in him, or had Old Coyote penetrated his very soul?

"You heard in the council how Orontondi left this country to settle in Saundustee," Reynard began. "The reason he left was because he grew tired of the French and the way they treated the People. He is trading with the English there."

"But what has this got to do with me?" Adelle asked. "The Indians and the French have always worked together."

"The time for peace may have passed. When I traded with the French traders in the area, they talked freely among themselves. They think a Wendat cannot understand their language. They are so ignorant," he scoffed. "They talk of the French commandant, DeLongueuil. He is upset over Orontondi trading with the English."

"He should be," Adelle spoke up. "And you had a dream that Orontony was killed. It is only a dream."

"That is where you are wrong. Dreams tell the future; they reveal truth. My oki has spoken with that of the spirits to give me this wisdom. And you can help me. You see there were letters– letters I could not read, but you–"

"Me?" Adelle cried. "How could I possibly get hold of one of DeLongueuil's letters?" She was incredulous that he could even imagine such a thing. "It is against the law! No, I cannot help you. I am going to Pontchartrain. That is where I was headed when you found me. No. I cannot," she repeated, shaking her head. She folded her arms, pressing them against her stomach. A wave of ausea swept over her, and her heart beat faster.

Reynard stepped in front of her. "It is not a matter of what you want. It is a matter of what is best for you. The people of the lake country are talking war. Tre-zue! No white will be safe. I brought you here as a Wendat for your own safety, not out of any respect for you, but as a debt I owe your father. I would have brought you with me anyway; your father would have agreed to it, at length. He would have realized you needed your mother's family. But I was prepared to take you even if he had not. Now it does not matter. I need someone to read those letters, and you will."

"My mother was from Montreal. What are you talking about? You would have taken me from my father by force?" The sound of her voice seemed strange in her ears. She spoke the last in a whisper, barely able to form the words.

"He would have given you."

She laughed lightly. "You are crazy." Papa would have done no such thing, she thought.

"No. He would have understood what I am saying so plainly, unlike you who do not because you are a child. Che-ah-hah." His tone was mocking, condemning.

Adelle's face flushed with anger. She wanted to lash at him with her knife but her sheath was empty. "You are a stinking Huron dog, Reynard DuPree! You are turning your back on your father's blood. If I did read those letters, how do you know I would tell you the truth?"

"I would not know, mademoiselle. I would have to trust you."

Adelle blinked at his calm reply.

"I wish you no harm," he said. "I speak the truth when I say you are safer as a Wendat. I speak the truth when I say if you help me, I will bring you back to Pontchartrain as soon as it is possible." Reynard waited for her response, and when there was none, he took a step back. "I also speak the truth when I tell you, you are safer if you stay with me. I want nothing of you but to read the letters."

"Stay with you? What do you mean, 'Stay with you?' " Adelle demanded.

"Big Hawk Flying, the young brave at the council, thinks you would make a good wife." He tapped his chest. "Strong eiachia; great bravery and fire. He has asked to have you if I change my mind."

"You wouldn't–"

"I do not know." Reynard shrugged.

Adelle did not doubt in his twisted thinking this would be an honorable thing to do. "You had this whole thing planned!" She poked her finger at his bare chest. "You probably asked Big Hawk if he wanted a wife."

"You over estimate my cruelty, mademoiselle. I would never ask of Big Hawk Flying such a trial. Surely he would end up trading you the first chance he got. He would find, as I have, that you are far more trouble than you are worth."

Reynard turned to go. "Tomorrow I am leaving for Saundustee. There is a trading post to the south that receives letters from Pontchartrain regularly. I will not tie you again. The choice is yours. If you decide to run away, I will take that to mean you do not wish to be with me, and I will send Big Hawk Flying to search for you. He is young and eager. I am certain he would find you. Marie might let you stay with her? But I doubt it. You would be on your own."

She watched him walk back toward the village until he disappeared behind the green, leafy veil of willows. Like a snake into his hole, she thought. Her moccasins sank into the damp sandy earth as she walked to the water's edge. She crouched there, dangling her fingers in the clear, cool water. She had no intention of becoming Big Flying Whatever's wife, and she believed Reynard would make good his threat if she ran away.

Across the pond, the sun shone like a beam from heaven on two maples, a gleaming lemon and a shining crimson. "God where are You?" she asked out loud. She felt the heaviness inside her like a dark curtain drawn over her heart. "Why have You brought me here?"

Had not Papa said that God has only love for His children? Had she not become His child? Adelle watched the rippling rings on the pond as droplets fell from her raised fingers onto the water below. As long as she could remember she believed that Jesus died on the cross to save all men's sins, and she trusted in this Christ as Papa had taught her. Her heart ached at the thought of Papa.

Adelle felt alone, so very alone in a vast wilderness teeming with enemies and men with well laid plans. There was no one who even expected her in Pontchartrain. She raised her head, tears blurring the trees against the white-blue sky. "God, You are all I have. If You love me, then show Yourself to me. If You care–" She choked a sob. "If You care, then show me what to do." She bowed her head and let the tears come freely. She did not care to hold them back anymore.

Adelle sat a long while in the silence of the autumn woods, remembering the time she had spent with Jesuits at the mission in St. Joseph while Papa traded near there. They had been pleased to teach her, to have a willing student. Sacrifice, they had taught her; sacrifice yourself, your will to God's.

"You have brought me here, God, have you not? What is it that You ask of me? What is Your will?"

A chickadee flitted from limb to limb in the tree above her. "Dee-dee-dee," it called down to her, its black cap shining in a ray of sun. She stretched out her arm, and the bird landed on the back of her hand, its tiny feet only a delicate caress against her skin. In the forest everything worked together. God controlled it all. Nothing was too small to be of worth; nothing was so big it was independent of His care. The chickadee darted away. Somehow God was in control of all these things happening to her, she thought. A calmness, not actually peace, settled deep inside her. Fear of the unknown hindered her assurance, but despite a desire for the contrary, a conviction was forming in her heart.

The afternoon was fading into early evening as Adelle walked back to the Huron village. Reynard sat with Old Coyote, but he rose to meet her as she made her way through a circle of playing children.

"I will go with you," she said. "But you must take me to Pontchartrain by summer."

"You have my word," Reynard replied, and Adelle believed him.

In the morning they loaded Reynard's large canoe with supplies. Marie smeared Adelle's hair with bear grease and tied it back like her own. She gave her a wrap around deerskin skirt that tied at the waist and a blouse type garment that fit over her head made from the same soft hide. Red and brown quillwork decorated the hemline of the skirt and across the bodice and shoulders of the blouse. A trio of necklaces was draped around her neck. Marie fastened a shell brooch to Adelle's collar and wrapped a fingerwoven sash around her waist. She attached Chaboillier's knife sheath to the sash and handed her his knife.

"A woman is known by what she provides her family," Marie said as Adelle fingered the fringe of her sash.

"These are beautifully done, Marie," Adelle complimented her.

Marie smiled. "I do not speak to gather your praise, but to give you knowledge. You will be expected to provide for the other families in your longhouse as well as yourself. Older women are your aneheh, mother. Listen and obey them."

Adelle nodded and took the leggings and moccasins Marie offered her. These too were decorated in the same fashion as her blouse and skirt, with the quillwork running down the center front seam of the leggings and on the wing flaps of her moccasins. The moccasins were dyed black in the fashion of the Iroquois.

"I have never worn anything so beautiful," Adelle admitted, running her fingers over the extensive embroidery.

Marie tossed Adelle's French trader's clothes and moccasins in a wooden chest under her bunk.

"There is one more thing," Marie said, taking a sharp instrument from a basket.

Adelle blinked. It was a needle, or small knife of some sort, for working animal hides.

"Sit," Marie commanded handing her two strings of white shells.

Adelle stiffened as she realized what Marie intended to do. She was about to cut her ears as all Indian mothers did to their babies soon after birth. If Adelle were to appear as a Wendat woman, then she must fully look the part. She sat perfectly still as Marie worked the knife, and a painful burning stung her ears. Carefully, Marie threaded the strings of shells through the holes as Adelle held her breath. The strings smelled of herbs, and Adelle realized they were greased with some type of salve.

Finally, she looked down at herself and wiped the blood from her ears. No one would ever recognize her as Adelle Chaboillier, she thought.

"Come," Marie said.

Outside the sky was overcast, and a chill wind swept through the village. Adelle tried her best to control the anxiety and dread that tempted her to run, run far from this place. This whole predicament was not of her choosing. Her will fought it with every step she took. She felt weak as the war raged within her. The temptation to give in to what she desired, and on the other hand to obey the Voice whispering in her heart, was indeed a war.

She climbed into the canoe and grabbed the paddle leaning against a thwart. While Reynard pushed off, she peered over her shoulder for one last look at the vast forest beyond the shore. She may never see Papa's little trading post again. She may not ever get to Pontchartrain. She swallowed the cry rising in her throat. Determined not to look back again, she turned and held her chin high. Her only hope was that the God, the Creator of her life, would gift her with the strength to carry out whatever it was He wanted her to do. She tightened her hand over the grip of her paddle and slid her other hand down its shaft.

Soon they turned into the wider waters of Rivière aux Hurons and from there onto the lake. The wind rolled the water to shore in an undulating mosaic of indigo grey and silver. The rain began as a white mist across the lake and fell as soft as fog on Adelle's face and hands. The sun, a creamy white glow, shone through a break in the smoke colored clouds. As the sunlight fell on the water ahead, it created a sparkling path for their bark canoe. Adelle drank in the beauty surrounding her, and a spark of hope ignited in the depths of her heavy heart. Her God was going with her.

Twenty-five year old Jean Baptiste stood calmly before the French commandant, DeLongueuil. "You asked to see me, Sir?"

"Yes, Monsieur Baptiste. I have need of a loyal French citizen with certain uh, how shall I say, capabilities, yes? Your presence here in Pontchartrain has been greatly appreciated by the governor general. He is grateful for your work with Chief Macinac and for assisting the French raids into British territory. Your repeated loyalty to New France has been brought to my attention, and what I am about to tell you must not pass through these doors." DeLongueuil eyed him carefully.

Jean Baptiste hid his surprise at the urgency of the commandant's tone. He was impatient to hear the rest. "Agreed, Sir," he answered.

"Very well then. The Huron chief, Orontony, whose baptized name is Nicholas, has been trading with the British. Reports are coming in that he has permitted the construction of a British trading post in his village and is allowing British trade with other tribes in the area." DeLongueuil paced behind his desk, his tone evidence of his opinion of the matter.

"I realize this may be common knowledge to a man like yourself, but now English traders from Pennsylvania are penetrating into the farthest reaches of New France to undercut our commerce. Also, some Virginians have rallied together to advance English settlement in the Ohio Valley. This is most upsetting. The British desire a foothold in New France, and Chief Nicholas is opening the way." DeLongueuil stopped pacing and folded his arms across his chest.

"Here is where you can help us," he said. "We need someone to act as an informant among the tribes in Chief Nicholas's territory. We need to know how the people of this area think, how Chief Nicholas is persuading them and what is the best way to put an end to his influence. You, Monsieur Baptiste," DeLongueuil pointed, "since you are half Outawae with a good reputation among both Indian and French, seem to be that someone."

DeLongueuil sighed. "It is very dangerous. It may cost you your life. It could mean torture at the hands of Nicholas if you are discovered as a spy. There you have it." He held up his hands then let them fall into a folded clasp at his waist in the manner of military dignity that so suited him.

Jean Baptiste pressed his lips together thoughtfully. "How long until you need an answer?" he asked after several minutes.

"As soon as possible. It is rumored that Nicholas is calling tribes to council."

"I will come tomorrow and give my answer."

"Very good then." DeLongueuil walked him to the door. "Think it over well. It is a decision that is most grave."

"Commandant." An officer saluted him at the threshold. "The company from the Fox territory has returned."

DeLongueuil nodded. "Very well," he answered the officer. He turned back to Jean. "Tomorrow then," he said, dismissing him.

"Tomorrow," Jean replied and stepped out into the cool autumn breeze. A cold drizzle fell from the grey sky. He could see the smoke rising in wisps from the Jesuit's house next to the church. He walked towards it, a familiar stop on his way to his father's farm just outside the fort. He would visit his friend, Father Francois today. He would stop and hear what wisdom his God would speak through the mouth of the Jesuit.

Adelle and Reynard pulled to shore as the last streaks of light painted the sky. The rain had delayed them a bit, but the night sky promised a clear day to come. Adelle found dry wood for a fire, and Reynard cleaned the fish he had caught. She stood by drying her clothes as he roasted their supper. Their stomachs full, their bodies warmed, they made their plans.

"Fort Miamis is two days behind us." Reynard gestured to the southwest. "We will wait along the Maumee for passing traders. They should be coming from Pontchartrain soon when DeLongueuil sends out his messengers. I know a spot where we can watch the river and the trails."

Adelle watched the shadows of the lake in the fading light. The glories of autumn were fading as nature donned the brown coat of November, and soon the lake would become choppy with winter winds.

"How will you get these letters, Reynard? These men are not idiots. They will be carrying them in their coat."

Reynard shrugged. "I will know when the time comes."

"This is all so ridiculous," Adelle sneered. "There is probably nothing in those letters, but supply orders and gossip."

"We will see then, will we not?" Reynard was undaunted.

"It is almost November. Winter will be upon us. Your sky oki may not favor you when you travel the lake again," Adelle warned.

"If the weather stays clear, it will be well."

"If not?"

Reynard settled into his pile of furs. "Then we will know we must work harder."

"I thought Indians were superstitious," Adelle mocked him.

"Some are." Reynard met her sarcasm smoothly. "But they are not as determined as I am."

Adelle threw down a mat for herself. It annoyed her that he had calm ready answers. "How do you know I will not take the canoe and leave you here after you have fallen asleep?"

Reynard chuckled slyly. "Chaboillier was an honest man. I trust he raised a daughter who is true to her word."

"Trust can be a dangerous thing, no?" She drew her blanket up to her chin to keep out the night chill.

Reynard rose up on his elbow and stared at her through the hissing fire. His black eyes emitted a strength of authority that melted the next taunt forming on her lips.

"Trust is life or death, mademoiselle," he said quietly. "Trust the wrong person and you die. Trust the right person and you have a friend who brings life to you. You must decide which person I am."

Adelle could not hold his gaze. Reynard lay back down, and she watched the flames for a long time. She wanted to hate him, but little by little, this strange man was beginning to intrigue her.

They awoke to clear skies, and Reynard desired to put as much shore behind them as possible. They paddled all day, eating pemmican and dried meat to sustain them. Adelle's arm muscles were stiff with pain, and her legs felt cramped.

"I have to rest again," she told Reynard over her shoulder. She slid the paddle beside her as she reached into her bag for more dried corn.

"Stretch," Reynard told her. "I will hold it steady." Briefly he held his paddle still.

Adelle obeyed him, relieving her tight leg muscles. She returned to a kneeling position slowly, and a movement along the shoreline caught her eye. Three Indian women stood on the bank.

"Reynard," Adelle whispered nervously. "Over there."

Reynard followed her gaze, his paddle never hesitating. "Keep going, unless I tell you otherwise."

Adelle stroked the water calmly with her paddle, trying not to stare as they passed by. The women were probably used to strangers passing through, but there was always a chance their village braves would prevent them from doing so. The memory of Papa's dead body flashed vividly in her mind. Adelle shuddered in spite of herself.

"Miamis," Reynard said when they were well out of sight. "They follow Orontondi as their chief and are very testy concerning the French. We will speak only Wendat now. You will learn more of the language."

He seemed such a hard man, and yet this duty he felt to keep her alive. She did not believe it was only for what she could do for him. He had admitted his debt to her father. Obviously this kindness of Papa's had cast a lasting influence that was a soft spot in an otherwise jagged rock of a soul. Could he possibly be sympathetic towards her, an orphan? She raised her eyebrows.

"How do you say, 'Do you miss your father' in Wendat?" she asked innocently.

Reynard answered slow enough for her to repeat it, and then corrected her halting effort.

"Well do you?"

"What?" He was annoyed by her play.

"Do you miss your father?" she asked in Huron trying to stifle her French accent.

"My father is Old Coyote."

"I mean your real father."

But Reynard did not answer.

"Do you believe in God?" she tried again.

He laughed heartily. “So you have spent time with the Black Robes?”

Adelle watched him over her shoulder. “Some, yes. Is that so funny?”

He laughed again. “If you know them as I do.”

“How is that?”

“As fools,” Reynard replied, unsmiling. “Fools to think they can ever change the People. They speak against the separation of a woman and a man, but they refuse to see it is Wendat life.”

“Separation?”

“If a Wendat is unhappy in their marriage, they may choose another.”

“Oh.” Adelle frowned.

“There are other things they will never change. The way of the young woman and the young man. A Wendat is not bound to purity as the whites until they choose a mate. These are the ways that have become the People. They will not easily be forgotten.”

“But should they not be?”

“It depends at whose fire you sit.”

“Where do you sit?” she asked.

“And the brandy,” Reynard continued, ignoring her question. “The Black Robes speak against the brandy while their French brothers offer it freely as a gift. Fools!”

“I believe in God.”

“And good for you!” he shot back.

“But your own father was French. Do you have no respect for him and his beliefs?”

“Enough!” Reynard shouted. “I wish to hear no more of your idle noise. I brought you along to read, not preach. Shut up and paddle!”

By the look on his face, Adelle thought it best to do as he said. But, she decided, this conversation was far from being over. That afternoon they reached the shores of the Maumee, and Reynard settled them inland at a point above the river. He sat patiently waiting for her while she searched for wood to make a fire that would not smoke. Then she cleaned the fish she caught and tossed the bones into the flames.

Reynard jumped to his feet. "Stop!" he thundered, snatching the knife away from her.

Adelle fell backward, partly from shock, partly from fear.

"A Wendat would never abuse the animal that feeds them!" He picked the bones from the coals. "If you disrespect their corpse they will tell the living animals who will not allow themselves to be caught. You will remember this!" Reynard thrust the knife into the sand at her feet.

How could I forget? Adelle thought. His moodiness frightened her. But she said nothing and shakily retrieved her knife. The rest of the night was spent in silence. Adelle covered herself with Marie's sleeping robe and watched through half closed lids as Reynard sat brooding into the fire. In the morning, she went down to the river and caught a fish for their breakfast. This time she threw the bones into the forest.

Pierre Antoine stirred the ashes of the fire one last time to make sure no sparks remained. He lifted his gun to his shoulder and nodded to the man with him.

"We must travel carefully from here," the man said in French despite his Pouteaouatami accent. "Miamis will be watching as we pass through their lands. It would be easier to travel the river." The man seemed to be accusing Pierre.

Pierre nodded again. "Yes, you said that yesterday. But I told you I want to avoid the post there. It would only delay us." His companion didn't seem convinced. "Let's get started," Pierre said, avoiding the Indian's suspicious stare.

Pierre followed his hired guide down the trail. St. Joseph lay far behind them to the northwest, and before them lay the rich land of the Erie basin–sometimes dangerous land, sometimes friendly. It all depended on the mood of the Indians living there. He speculated on the mood of the Indian.

In spite of his companion, Pierre paced himself for the long trek they would make that day. He felt good to be on the trail of opportunity. His enthusiasm failed slightly as he thought of the consequences that might come as a result of the actions he took to get there. But he shrugged off the nuisance of guilt.

The sun was low in the afternoon sky when they reached the waters of the Maumee. "We will stop here for the night," the Indian informed him.

Wearily, Pierre dropped the canoe to the ground. Carrying the supplies overland was foolish when there was a water route, he thought. But he could take no chances. He stretched his neck and shoulders. Someone might recognize him despite his fur trader's clothing. Tomorrow they would be taking a shorter portage south.

Soon a fire blazed, and meat cooked over the flames. Pierre relaxed in the evening sun, the worst part of the journey behind him. The Indian speared a hunk of fish with his knife and ate it slowly, watching Pierre across the tops of the flames.

"A story was told to me," he said, "of a French soldier lost in a Fox raid. He was never found. Captured, his friends said." He wiped his knife blade on his leggings. "But none of the People talk of this soldier. I ask myself, why would a Fox take a white without killing him? What benefit would it be for them if they did not gloat on his torture?" He watched the flames lick the wood before going on. "Unless the man disappeared on his own."

Pierre stared hard into the fire. The Indian's words had hit their mark. It did not really matter. It would not be long until he reached the Guyahauga. Then he would not need a guide.

The Indian spread a mat on the ground and lay down. Pierre watched the twilight sky, the first star of the night shining against a pink glow. Soon he would rid himself of this bothersome Indian, he thought darkly.

Three days went by before a French party in a dugout passed below them. Reynard tensed at the sight before him, melting into the woods like the yellow panther stalking a deer.

Adelle sat on the rise, well hidden, and prayed for the Tu-hew-car-o-no, the Frenchman's life and his two employees. She had no idea how Reynard planned to steal letters the man may be carrying, but she knew nothing would stop him from trying. She fully believed he would kill these men if he had to.

She strained to hear any sound that would indicate a meeting between the men. The wind swayed the tops of the trees and creaked the limbs overhead. The water spilled over itself in a symphony of gurgles, bubbles and tinkles as it flowed below her, but she could detect nothing else.

Adelle ran to where she could see the bend in the river and stood biting her lip. She searched the water frantically, and finally the men in the canoe floated by, unaware that Reynard was only about five canoe lengths behind, hid among the trees. He continued upriver, and Reynard stealthily followed.

Later, she ate supper alone, or at least she tried to eat. Instead of the stomach-stretching end of the day affair it usually was, her meal was more akin to choking down her food because that is what time of day it was, and that is what one did: eat. She needed something to do to keep her busy, and she relied on routine to prevent her mind from turning its evil progression of thoughts into a tangling web of fear.

Fear. Fear that Reynard would not come back, and fear that he would. Her mind ran with this continuous thought so long she was rigid with anxiety. The stars appeared one by one like snowflakes on velvet in the black sky. She lay under her sleeping robe, shifting this way and that, never able to make herself comfortable. Wolves sang their mournful songs in the night air. At other times Adelle would be comforted by the sad yet peaceful notes, but tonight they grated against her raw nerves to the point she feared going mad.

She closed her eyes only to be tormented by ghastly visions: Reynard with his gleaming knife in the firelight, Papa collapsed in a pool of his own blood, wolves circling, pacing to get the letter she clutched in her hand.

Adelle thrust her eyelids open wide. Someone was near. She didn't know why she knew, but she knew. She drew Papa's knife from her belt and held the corner of her sleeping robe. She was ready to explode into action any second. The wolves had stopped howling, and the forest was quiet, too quiet.

She cursed the pounding of her heart in her ears as she strained to hear the slightest movement. Suddenly Reynard appeared towering over her. She leaped from her bed and screamed, releasing all the fear coursing through her body out through her lungs.

Reynard clamped a warm hand over her mouth and pressed his arm against her throat. "Idiot!" he rasped in her ear.

Adelle gasped for breath as he loosened his hold on her. A thin strip of pink tinted the eastern sky. He pulled out a white roll of paper from his coat.

"Are they dead?" she croaked rubbing her Adam's apple.

"Dead? Am I a fool? I do not want DeLongueuil's men crawling the forest like ants."

"How did you get it then?"

Reynard looked at her as if she were utterly stupid beyond all hope. "I waited for them to fall asleep. Then I walked up and took it while they lay there snoring. Read it." He handed her the paper.

She knelt by the cold fire and slid her finger under the seal. What might happen to her if the French discovered she conspired with an Indian against her own country she wondered. What might happen to her countrymen if she gave away information that put them in danger?

"Read it!" Reynard nudged her roughly. He was tired of waiting.

She broke the seal. "British are offering peltry for French scalps–" Adelle's voice died away. "God, have mercy on us," she breathed.

"Read." He nudged her again.

"DeLongueuil is warning the posts and asking them to warn French traders. He wants to stop Chief Nicholas's dealings with the English."

"Hmph! How will he do it?"

"It doesn't say any more."

Reynard stuffed the paper into his coat. "It is time to go." He tramped through the white, frost-covered grass and picked up the canoe.

Adelle hastily rolled the sleeping mat and robe and followed him down to the river. She paddled solemnly all morning. Her arms moved automatically. She was tired and deeply troubled. When the sun was high, she divided the baked corn between them.

"The British are asking for French scalps." She twisted around to face him, handing him the leather pouch with the rest of the corn in it. "My scalp, Reynard. And you are carrying me into Orontony's very lap. The man who hates the French. And you think I am safer?" Her voice rose with each word. "Do you think they are not going to notice I am French? You call me an idiot!"

Reynard glanced at her. He took a mouthful of corn and resumed paddling. "You forget who I am."

"The great warrior, Mighty Fox," Adelle taunted, sarcastically.

Reynard shook his head. "I should have left you at the Maumee." He shifted his paddle to the other side. "I am Old Coyote's son, and I will keep you safe until we return to Pontchartrain. Then it is up to you."

"The English are only asking you to kill us to further themselves in trade and land, not to benefit the People. Don't you understand this?"

"The People will do what is best for them, and when it is time. If the snake asks the bear to kill the fox, then all that is left for the bear to do is kill the snake. It would be harder for the bear to kill them both at once. First he must eliminate one, then the other."

Adelle sucked on her corn thoughtfully. Had this whole affair been thought through that far? Did the Pontchartrain Huron believe that once they rid their land of the French they would be able to do the same with the British? If what Reynard said was true, the British sure had a shock coming. She turned around again and pulled her paddle through the water. Only time would reveal if any of these things could be accomplished.

Aanii!" Jean Baptiste greeted his cousin, Rising Sky, an Odawa brave who was waiting for him in the Odawa village on the shore of the Erie.

"Aanii," Rising Sky returned and flashed a smile. "Anish -na-ezhiyaayin?" he asked.

"Niminoyaa gwa," Jean answered to his condition and pointed to the canoe. "Gizhiitawshin?"

"En'," Rising Sky affirmed, reaching for a paddle.

Jean Baptiste sprang lightly into the canoe behind Rising Sky and grabbed the paddle offered to him. They were travelling north to Waganawkezee, L'Arbre Croche in French. His father, wishing to settle his family in a place where they could experience the benefits of French culture, had moved them to the Odawa village north of Pontchartrain when Jean was older. Jean, like his father, had no trouble establishing himself as a man of honor, for he was well-liked and often called upon to negotiate with the French on their behalf. Now, despite his real mission, that of acting as an informant for DeLongueuil, he felt no guilt staying among the People to listen to their councils and to act as their friend, for in his heart he was. He held no loyalty to the French, a fact that would have surely shocked DeLongueuil. The truth was he held no loyalty to any man, only to that which was right. Men changed opinion and fealty; God did not.

He was thankful he had learned the importance of living at a higher standard than most choose for themselves. He had learned from a young age not to take his heritage, the mixing of cultures, as a hindrance but an advantage. He was thankful he was not limited to one insight but was able to see a larger image of life. He was something new, he thought, born of this time and this place. Today he would listen and make his judgment based on the Wisdom that had formed the earth and cast the stars in the heavens.

The sun broke through the clouds, warming the men as they cut the water with their paddles. They were travelling with other Odawa and Anishinaabe braves to Chief Twisted Bark's village. Chief Nicholas had sent his wampum stick to them also, and the People would come together in council to decide their position on the matter of war. It was no secret that the reason Chief Nicholas left Pontchartrain was because of disputes with the Odawa and his fear of their anger. But today, old rivalries were put aside to join together against a common enemy.

"Mizhakwad," another brave named Lone Stump called to Jean and Rising Sky from his canoe. He was referring to the good weather.

"En'," Rising Sky agreed with a wide grin. "It is good for us, bad for the wemitigoozhi!"

Lone Stump laughed. "Daga bin," he cautioned. "Msko-aki-bmibtood, ayaa!"

Please be careful he had said. Red Earth Runner is behind you. Jean smiled at the mention of his Odawa name, Red Earth Runner, and his cousin pretended to duck as he glanced back over his shoulder. Wemitigoozhi, the French. Jean was often teased about his heritage, but it was never meant as a rebuke, or spoken of with contempt, for the Ojibwa named his father Dabwewan, meaning he was one to be trusted.

But Jean knew Rising Sky was serious in his reference to the French, and the general opinion was the same: the French noos, father, had proven to be greedy and spiteful. He was requiring more and more pelts for trade goods. This was not the actions of an Odawa father toward his children. Jean understood their grievances. To the contrary, the British had no license fees or regulations to hinder their trade, so they were able to offer goods at much lower prices. The Odawa were weary of the demands made upon them by the French. Obliterating them from their territory seemed an easy solution.

He paddled silently, listening to the excited banter of his companions. In the next few days, Twisted Bark and the elders would relate to them what the Odawa had chosen, to unite with Orontony or not. Jean studied the Odawa braves with him as they paddled deliberately and passionately toward Twisted Bark. On their lips were smiles, in their eyes resolution. Jean already knew what the Odawa's answer would be. War. His heart quickened, and he wondered again what this trip might cost him.

The weather remained in Reynard's and Adelle's favor, and they continued paddling as the lake curved east. The time was spent repeating words in Wendat, a task Adelle took seriously since she believed her life depended on it.

A hardy Frenchman could travel a hundred miles in a day, more if he paddled through the night. But a determined Wendat could probably do better than that, Adelle decided. They neared Saundustee that afternoon, and the wind began to pick up. Reynard had switched positions with her. Apparently he did not trust her judgment when it came to watching for ripples that were hidden rocks along this stretch of dark, rough water.

"We will not make it to the bay in time. A storm is coming. We must pull in," Reynard told her as the spray from the lake began freezing on their clothes. "The lake oki knows we are here!" he shouted over the pounding waves, maneuvering the canoe with all the skill he possessed.

Adelle was too nervous to acknowledge his words. She obeyed the directions he shouted to her, hoping she had enough strength in her arms to hold to the course he wanted. She had heard of canoes breaking apart and men dying before they could be pulled from the frigid water or swept into the pull of unseen currents. She had no desire to experience it herself.

"Hard to the right!" Reynard directed her. "Hard to the right!"

Adelle tried to hold her position. When she felt for sure they would be dashed against the relentless waves or layers of jagged black rock, Reynard jumped into waist high water and guided them to shore.

"Ahh-Hee!" Reynard cried, maybe from excitement, maybe from the freezing cold water.

Silently forming a thankful prayer, Adelle splashed to shore over the slippery rocks. Reynard bent over with his hands resting on his knees. He smiled at her, his face dripping water, his teeth white against his skin.

"The oki was in our favor, yes?" He grinned.

He looked almost handsome. She smiled back. Her first genuine smile.

He stood up and was thoughtful for a minute. "There." He pointed. A faint curl of smoke rose above the trees in the distance. He gathered the packs from the canoe and handed them to Adelle. "You need to carry these," he said and turned away.

She dropped one on the ground when she struggled to shoulder the other. "What do I do, just walk in?" she demanded.

"Don't be foolish," he answered quickly. "You will speak only when someone speaks to you. If you do not understand, speak nothing. I will answer for you." He motioned for her to pick up the dropped pack.

"You will do as you see other women doing and respect them. Listen," he said, shaking his finger at her like a father admonishing a little child. "You must say you are from the mud turtle clan. Your mother's name was Blue Flowers, and she is dead. This is important." He paused making sure he had her attention. "Wendat heritage comes from the mother, not the father. The rest you can fill in yourself."

He shouldered the canoe. "Your Wendat name is Little Turtle."

"Little Turtle?" Adelle screwed her face into a disagreeable frown.

Reynard smiled. "A warrior's strong armor on the outside, but a soft belly underneath." He laughed at his own joke. He held up his hand as Adelle was about to lead the way. "If anyone asks, you are my wife."

"Don't be foolish," Adelle echoed him.

"I am serious." And by the look in his eye, she could tell that he was. "It is the only way to dispel suspicion," he went on, "and to avoid any curious young braves at the same time."

A picture of Big Hawk Flying flashed across her mind. Still, she was doubtful. "What does being your wife actually mean?"

"Nothing to me, I assure you," he said and pushed ahead of her into the brush.

The walk to the village was not an easy one. Cold rain poured from the sky. There was no river to carry them, and the wind whipped the trees together as they slipped over the soggy leaves of the forest floor. Adelle felt like her legs were made of warm milk.

Reynard stopped. "We must get to the village before dark," he told her. "Can you do this?"

"What if I can't?" she retorted, spitefully.

Reynard shot her a disgusted look. "You will." He trudged on through the trees. "If you have the energy for idiocy, then you have the energy to walk."

Adelle stood there, the rain streaming down her face. She felt shamed by his rebuke. He had tried to be nice to her, and she had acted like a spoiled child. She hated to admit it, but she was sorry she had displeased him. She followed after him, her legs aching and her shoulders throbbing with the weight of both packs. Reynard seemed to sense her fatigue and quickened the pace. It did cross her mind he did this to punish her, but she remembered Papa would often do the same thing.

"Adelle," he would say, "if you slow down, you will stop. You must put one foot in front of the other."

She forced herself to go on as Papa had taught her, and she felt stronger because of it. The shore soon curved to the west. Farther up the beach Wendat canoes rested on the yellow sand. Reynard stopped. An Indian was coming down the path. Adelle's stomach fluttered, and her heart began to beat faster.

Reynard glanced at her. "I am Mighty Fox," he told her, "son of Old Coyote."

Adelle nodded. He was reminding her not to call him by his French name and, Adelle took a deep breath, that he would protect her. She walked behind him, keeping her eyes fixed on his back, his wide shoulders. For some reason, she knew it now, God had brought them together, and whatever happened next was in His plan.

Providence

"A-en-ye ha!" The brave cried who had come to meet them. He called Reynard brother, but Adelle decided he wasn't. They looked nothing alike.

He was tall with a long sloping nose that had a good sized bump just below the bridge, a notable feature for the Wendat. His lips were full, and his chin protruded to a point that balanced his large nose. His head was shaved on one side, the remaining hair hanging loose and gleaming with a coat of animal fat. She could smell it.

"Running Dog!" Reynard smiled, even with his eyes. Obviously he was a good friend.

Adelle wondered why a man of his bearing should be burdened with such an insulting name. But their names were symbolic, she reminded herself. Perhaps the words running dog referred to the wolf who had a higher stature among the Indian people than a dog.

"Scan-dai-ye?" Are you married, the brave inquired, pointing to Adelle.

Reynard nodded. "Azut-tun-oh-oh." He introduced her as his wife.

Running Dog raised his eyebrows as he looked her over. "Ye-waugh-ste." Good, he said. "Owa." And he led the way along a path to the village about a mile inland, he and Reynard chatting about the trip and Old Coyote.

Soon they arrived, and Adelle thought the whole village must have come to greet them as Reynard seemed to be well-liked among these people. The same friendly chant surrounded them as before.

"Ho! Ho! Ho! Ho!" The village was alive with welcome.

A man limped toward them, his face grooved with many lines, but not soured as in old age, for the lines around his eyes made him appear to be smiling. His grey hair was long, and strands lifted by the wind brushed his gaunt, brown cheeks. He stopped in front of them, putting his hands on Reynard's shoulders.

"Mighty Fox," he greeted him. "My eyes have grown weary watching for you. My heart has grown heavy in your absence. Now, when I see you stand here among the People, my blood is new again."

Reynard rested his hands on the old man's shoulders in the same warm greeting. "Yellow Sun, you bring warmth to my spirit. There are many things I bring to you from my father, Old Coyote. I bring his gifts, and I bring the words of the Wendat to the great chief Orontondi."

Yellow Sun smiled, his toothless gums showing, a sparkle gleaming in his eye. He pointed to Adelle. "Old Coyote's gift to an aging man?" he said, chuckling.

Reynard smiled back. "This is my wife, Little Turtle. She is also of the mud turtle clan."

Yellow Sun turned to her, and Adelle hoped no one noticed her knees were literally shaking like the last trembling leaf dangling from a tree.

Raising his hand to her in a gesture of greeting, Yellow Sun beamed. "You are welcome in the home of Yellow Sun. What is your mother's name?"

"Blue Flowers," Adelle answered trying not to squeak.

The old man's smile slowly faded. Gravely he lowered his head. Had she said something wrong?

Finally he looked up and touched Reynard's chest with his thin, gnarled hand. "Come," he said after some hesitation. "We will celebrate your coming and the marriage of Mighty Fox and Little Turtle."

A feast was soon prepared in their honor, and Running Dog, the tall brave that had greeted them on the beach, brought Adelle a beautiful robe made of woven strips of rabbit fur. His wife, Shining Water, was shy and quiet with delicate features and a soft voice. Her dress was painted, and she wore dyed, fringed sashes at her waist. Adelle thought she was the prettiest woman she had ever seen and instantly took a liking to her, admiring her fine manners. But she was startled to discover Shining Water was probably a year, or two younger than she was.

Dog meat was roasted over the fires on sticks, and a drum beat joyously as young people danced around the large fire in the center of the village. They carried deerhorn rattles decorated with leather fringe and feathers, shaking them with precision. Soon it was the dance of the braves, and Reynard joined Running Dog and the others as they stomped the ground and pushed their heels into it. Almost a bouncing step, but lighter, and to the steady rhythm of the drums and rattles.

The firelight shone on their bronze faces which were streaked with dyes: purple, green, red and black. Their naked chests gleamed with perspiration as the dance wore on, and Adelle watched awed by the strength and power of these men. She imagined them fierce in battle against their enemy. But, she was their enemy.

Adelle fingered the rabbit fur robe folded in her lap. Nervously, she glanced sideways at Shining Water seated next to her, proudly watching Running Dog as he acted out his part of the dance.

To her right, Yellow Sun also observed the performance from his place near the fire. His young grandchildren flocked around him, their eager, round faces bright with excitement. The youngest little girl, perhaps six Adelle guessed, climbed into Yellow Sun's lap.

"Ug-gh!" he faked. "You are heavy like our brother the bear."

She giggled. "Tell us about Sky Woman again, Grandfather."

"The divine woman. In the beginning there was only water," Yellow Sun began, and all the children moved a bit closer to the fire in order to hear his mellow voice. "One day Divine Woman tumbled from the sky and two loons caught her, saving her from a death of drowning." His voice lowered, full with the tease of suspense, as the story continued.

"The loons called upon the other animals to help them, for there was one water, and they did not know what to do with Sky Woman. Great Turtle advised the loons to place Sky Woman on her shell, and the other animals swam to the bottom of the great water and brought dirt to pile upon Great Turtle's back." Yellow Sun spread his arms wide. "This my children is how the earth was formed."

It was a creation legend, Adelle realized, as Yellow Sun went on to explain how the woman's sons made the animals. She couldn't help noticing his pride at the sight of his grandchildren's fascination with his tale. She knew, however, the importance of Yellow Sun's story, for this was their religion. And these stories were repeated often, not unlike the Jesuits who told and retold the Bible accounts. To Yellow Sun, the children's interest was a victory for the next generation of Wendat. It was a guarantee they would pass the stories on to their children, and the old ways would not be forgotten. It was a promise of their strength as a People in the future.

Suddenly Adelle became distracted by the growing frenzy of the dance. Surely Reynard must be the strongest one among them. He was built powerfully, and she watched, partly amazed, partly in disgust, as he twisted and whirled alongside the other men.

Across the leaping flames, Adelle could see a young man standing at a distance. He was tall, even for a Huron, with high chiseled cheekbones and the hooked nose and mohawked hair. His face was streaked with two diagonal red lines. A pair of owl claws hung at his neck. Silver arm bands flashed when he turned, and vertical lines were permanently tattooed on his stomach, beginning below his chest and ending above his waist. His skin was clear and bronze. A handsome Wendat, Adelle thought. His eyes were dark, not just in color, but from their countenance. His lips were full and gravely set. Truly, he must be one of their most powerful warriors, and yet he stood almost in loathing at the sight before him.

Adelle leaned close to Shining Water. "Who is the young brave that does not join in the dance?" she asked her.

Shining Water glanced in the young man's direction. "He is Brave Arrow, the war chief. He has much oki. But he is angered that Mighty Fox was chosen to carry the message of war. Brave Arrow says it is the job of the war chief, not a mètis."

Adelle nodded. She bit into the dog meat Shining Water offered her, and suppressed an impulse to gag. Oki was the Wendat word for gods or spiritual power. She swallowed the meat only to empty her mouth of it. She watched Brave Arrow again. Power. The word seemed to ooze from him. She followed his sullen gaze as he watched Reynard. Was it hate that made his eyes so dark? Adelle wondered.

The feast continued far into the night, and soon Reynard took her by the hand. Yips and shouts erupted from the Wendats as they walked back to Yellow Sun's longhouse. A drawing of a red turtle was etched into the wood pole above the door. Adelle looked back over the villagers. Darkness seemed to seep from the sky and drape itself over them. Darkness. Adelle repeated the word to herself. Reynard touched her shoulder, and she entered the longhouse.

A place had been sectioned off for them and another fire added to the center row. Someone had also laid a new sleeping robe for them on the platform built into the wall. Other smaller compartments flanked the sleeping platform and overhead like attic rooms. The middle section of the roof was left open for the smoke to escape, and drying fish and corn could be seen hanging from the cross poles. Reynard lay down on the platform.

"You must watch the dance next time and not another warrior," he said stretching out on the fur.

"I didn't know you noticed," she said pushing him over and pulling out a robe for herself. "You were too busy showing off."

He grabbed her braid and held it, pulling her head back. "I will notice anything a faithful Wendat woman would not do, and so will the others."

She pushed his hand away and lay down on the bark floor. Again she felt ashamed for treating his instruction with careless mockery. She studied the poles lashed together above her. "I-ye-et-sa-tigh." I am sorry, she finally whispered.

He rolled over on his side, and soon his even breathing told her he was asleep.

The days melted into a kind of comforting routine for Adelle. No longer was there a crisis for her to face each waking day as she had known since Papa's death. It was remarkably easy to pretend to be Wendat. She gathered acorns with Shining Water and the other women from her longhouse to grind into flour, ta-ish-ra. They gathered the last of the corn, nay-hah, pulling back the husks of each ear, tying them together in clusters and hanging them to dry on the longhouse crossbeams. Once it was dried, they stored it in wooden casks kept in the attic sections of the longhouse.

All the women in the longhouse were related, Adelle discovered. And all were from the mud turtle clan. Their husbands were of varying clans;

there were twelve in all: bear, wolf, deer, beaver, snake, porcupine, various turtles and hawk. It was not permitted to marry someone from your own clan. Each longhouse was inhabited by sisters and their daughters, and the oldest woman was the head of the family, rather than the oldest male.

Shining Water's aunt was the matron of their longhouse. She organized the work and divided the chores among the other women. She parceled out cooking, sewing and gathering chores, allotments for clan land to be planted in spring and advice to any who wished it, and to some who did not. The matrons chose the clan chiefs. What a difference there could be among tribes, Adelle marveled. In the Pouteaouatami and Outawae societies the men were responsible for everything it seemed but raising babies, gardening and cooking.

There were children in the longhouse as well, and the result was a kind of family-friendly chaos. To her own surprise Adelle enjoyed the company of these women. They became her sisters, mothers, aunts and grandmothers. It was the first time she had ever related to other women in a family setting, and it was comforting. They readily accepted her as Mighty Fox's wife, and she experienced a sense of belonging she had not felt in some time.

The men had already gone on long hunting trips for deer, bear and beaver. Now the women busied themselves preparing the hides, and the men assembled some of the furs to be traded. Reynard went on short fishing trips with the men, using nets made of hemp stretched across the narrow pass of the river. They put the nets in place at night, and in the morning they hauled in their catch. They also hunted turkeys.

The snows began, and soon the land was covered with its winter blanket. One crisp, sunny day when the dogs began to bark, Adelle went outside for she was well aware by now they signaled the arrival of visitors. She gazed across the clearing as Brave Arrow met three men wearing whiteman's clothes and carrying guns. But they were not whites.

"Iroquois traders," Shining Water said as she came up behind Adelle.

Brave Arrow led them to the chief's longhouse, and they disappeared through the opening.

Adelle and Shining Water returned to their work near the fire they shared. They sat on the ground rolling long hemp fiber strings back and forth against their legs with the palms of their hands. This action produced a strong twine.

The Iroquois were probably Brave Arrow's trading partners, Adelle thought. Many times Papa had travelled to the Pouteaouatami villages to trade with the men he had befriended. "How far do they travel?" she asked Shining Water, referring to the traders.

"Perhaps as far as Albany. The white traders are settled there. Their chief, Canassatego, agreed to give the whites the support of the Iroquois Confederacy if they would unite as one against the French almost three winters ago. Now they carry the white man's goods to us."

Adelle picked up more hemp strands for herself. "Mighty Fox has told me of the white trader's fair prices."

"Oh, but that is not all." Shining Water leaned forward, her dark brown eyes wide. "The Iroquois are urging us, the great chief Orontondi, to fight the French in Yondotin so their white father may prosper all the People."

Adelle stopped rolling. Attack Pontchartrain? "When will this happen?" she asked staring into her lap for fear Shining Water would see in her face the horror she felt.

"Orontondi is calling council to decide what the People desire to do. But he agrees with the Iroquois. He has gathered many nations to fight with him."

Adelle bit her lip. Frantically she called on her memory to produce the words Reynard had spoken to her about Orontony. She had been so concerned with herself she had not even considered the full impact of the events unfolding around her. This explained why Reynard had hid his canoe that fateful day. He needed to travel at night so his Saundustee presence near Pontchartrain would not arouse DeLongueuil's suspicions.

No wonder he was disappointed to see LeClere and he was angry the Miamis were acting impatiently by raiding Papa's post. He was worried they would give away the war. He had told Old Coyote of the council in her very presence. The wampum string he had given him was Orontony's invitation to war. Hadn't Shining Water told her the very first night that Reynard carried the message of war? No white will be safe, Reynard had said.

How stupid, how blind she had been, she thought disgustedly. Now she understood Reynard was not talking about raiding parties, but a full attack of organized proportion. Tre-zue, he had said. Anger burned in the pit of her stomach. He had wanted her to read those letters to find out if word of an uprising had reached DeLongueuil through gossiping Indian traders.

That night a bitterly cold wind howled through the treetops outside. She sat by their fire sewing deerskin into a pair of leggings, and Reynard relaxed across from her. They were alone in their compartment, an oddity in the life of the longhouse.

"Shining Water told me today that the Iroquois are urging the Wendat to attack Pontchartrain," Adelle said quietly. "Is this true?"

Reynard stared into the fire. "It is true," he answered evenly.

"Will the People do this?"

"Orontondi is a respected chief. His counsel will be regarded as wise."

"How many nations support him?"

"Miamis, Shawnee, Fox." He shrugged. "Some are only bands within these nations, but they are many."

Adelle leaned close to him so her words held no risk of being overheard. "You are forcing me to betray my countrymen to their deaths!"

"You have no faith in their ability then?" he said. "You should be thankful you are here among the Wendat."

"I would rather die with the French," she whispered through clenched teeth.

Reynard shrugged and said nothing more. The next morning, Adelle and Shining Water prepared baskets of dried corn for trade. The Iroquois were preparing to leave, and Yellow Sun had traded the corn for tobacco. Reynard came to the doorway of the longhouse as Shining Water was leaving with the last basket. He motioned for Adelle to come outside with him. She drew the rabbit fur robe around her, for outside the wind swirled the snow at her feet, and the sky was heavy with low grey clouds.

"Owa-he." Reynard motioned again. He walked some distance away from the other longhouses and busy villagers. "I am leaving with the Iroquois to visit Orontondi's village." He pointed west. "I will be gone maybe ten days."

"Ten days! Why?" Adelle felt her eyes widen.

"I will go with Running Dog. We will trade with the English and with the other villages. We will be welcomed, and we must honor their gifts to us."

She wanted to plead with him to stay with her or to let her go with him, but she said nothing. Especially not after her brave speech about rather dying with the French than being with his people. She only nodded, looking past him into the woods. She didn't want him to know she felt safer with him near her. She didn't want him to know she was afraid to be alone. But she was– terribly afraid. If anything happened to Reynard she would be stranded here. No matter how much she liked being part of their family, she was still French and the enemy.

"You knew yesterday; why didn't you tell me then?" she asked him. She kept her eyes on the trees behind him. She dared not look into his face, for the hardness there would surely have brought on tears of self pity.

"I will tell you when you need to know," he answered solemnly. "Get my supplies ready."

She was wrong, she thought. There was no soft spot in his soul. It was carved from duty only and what was needed to produce it. Adelle turned toward the village and started back along the path. She didn't feel like arguing with him. She was tired of his gruffness and hurt by his cold, unfeeling heart.

Slowly she entered the bustling longhouse. She put baked corn and pemmican in a leather pouch and folded Reynard's cloak over her arm. Her stomach fluttered at the thought of being alone. Then she remembered. It was not Reynard who was protecting her. It was the hand of her living God. Nothing could separate her from Him. Reynard came in and crossed the aisle to where she stood by their fire. He gave her only a passing glance as he took his things from her.

"Ten days," he repeated. He lingered.

Adelle looked up, her chin held high. It seemed he wanted to say something. But then he hung the pouch at his waist and walked out. Adelle didn't watch him leave. She shakily smoothed back her hair and busied herself making corn cakes for the families in her longhouse.

Orontondi's village was situated farther west near the mouth of the river that fed the bay. Reynard strode into the British post with Running Dog behind him. They had brought pelts to trade, and Reynard was eager to do business with them again.

A bad smelling Englishman stood by the entrance. "Hell-o!" Running Dog greeted him in halting English. But the man said nothing and spit a stream of brown juice on the ground behind him.

Reynard had never seen this man before. Neither had he seen the two Englishmen seated at the table inside. They sat one at either end with a bottle of rum between them and never looked up when he and Running Dog entered. Dirt smeared their chalky faces, and grime covered their necks and hands. Reynard grimaced. Unfortunately, the smell of rum did not cover their stench. One had yellow stringy hair with eyes the color of the sky, only they too seemed to be milky and weak. The other man was heavier with a good deal of hair the color of a bear, and he did look like one too, with his small dark eyes and a tuft of black hair at his throat.

"Hell-o!" Running Dog repeated, expecting the friendly response he had always received before.

Reynard scanned the room. No one else was inside. He became more indignant as the seconds passed, and still these men sat drinking and conversing with one another, never acknowledging him or Running Dog. Reynard wanted to clutch the bear-like man by his greasy collar and toss him from his chair. Finally, he slammed the pelts on the table in front of them, knocking over their rum.

"Here, here!" the pasty, yellow-haired man cried, jumping up to right the bottle. "That's good rum it is! Bloody savage wasting it like that!"

Bear-like man turned his head to look at Reynard. "Impatient one ain't he?"

Reynard did not understand what the words meant, but he knew from his tone that the hairy man mocked him. "We have come to trade," he informed them in Wendat.

Running Dog picked up his furs and handed them to The Weak One.

"Right, let's have a look at them," The Weak One said with a wave toward the goods on the counter.

Running Dog lifted a shiny, black rifle from the rack. Turning it over in his hands and admiring its quality, he grinned.

"No." The Weak One shook his skinny head. "No guns for trade." He crossed his hands thrust them out separating them again.

Running Dog put the gun down.

Reynard paid no more attention to the negotiations between Running Dog and The Weak One as he marveled how quickly the English attitude had changed toward them. It was only months ago the Wendat were respected for their foresight in dealing with the white traders from Albany and Pennsylvania. Apparently now that the whites had gotten their post, they were confident enough to insult the People.

Reynard watched as Bear Man closed his eyes and tipped the bottle to his waiting lips. In his heart he hated him. He knew Orontondi trusted these English. He trusted the word of their distant brother the Iroquois who were loyal English supporters. Bear Man wiped his mouth with the back of his filthy hand. Reynard blinked, and a seed of doubt fell into the soil of his heart.

Perhaps these men were the true kind of English traders and not just ignorant cast-offs that were left here. Perhaps there were more of these kinds of men waiting to fill the land after the honey-tongued, red-haired Pennsylvanian had secured the People's friendship. If these were the true English, he hated them more than the French.

Running Dog nudged him. It was time to go. He must not tell Running Dog his thoughts, for Running Dog was young yet, young in the way of the whites, and he would not understand.

The days passed quickly for Adelle, tempered by long prayers and her work on the sash she was making for Many-Small-Leaves, the young girl in the longhouse next to hers. The quillwork was not as good as Marie's but the challenge kept her interest. Adelle had separated the washed porcupine quills by size and had selected some to dye for the sash. Goldenrod, black walnuts, bloodroot and pokeberries gave the quills color: yellow, black, red and purple. But she found it tricky business to soften the quills in her mouth, draw them out between her teeth to flatten them and then wrap them around a single sinew thread to be sewn to the hide.

She wanted to give the sash as a gift for the girl's wedding that was soon to be celebrated since Brave Arrow had asked her parent's permission to propose. Many-Small-Leaves could deny him if she wished, but it was well known she desired his proposal. Soon on the day of his choosing, Brave Arrow would paint his face and bring Many-Small-Leaves a present. They would spend several nights together, but neither would be allowed to speak. When this was over, Many-Small-Leaves would decide if she accepted his proposal or not.

Many-Small-Leaves was also younger than Adelle, and Adelle wondered if Brave Arrow was a wise choice for her. She smiled to herself. She was beginning to think like Papa.

Shining Water gave her a curious glance. She sat next to Adelle sewing a tiny tunic. Shining Water had pounded the hide to amazing softness and with an awl had perforated the holes necessary for the needle stitches. For her it was quick work. She smiled, holding up the half finished garment. Her stitches seemed flawless, Adelle thought ruefully, but she smiled back. Shining Water was pregnant and due to have her baby during the summer. It was hard not to catch the pride and excitement fairly oozing from Shining Water's radiant face. A sudden fit of hoarse coughing could be heard at the other end of the longhouse where Yellow Sun rested close to his fire.

"He never seems to get warm this winter." Shining Water shook her head, lowering the little tunic to her lap. "He has aged with the snows. My mother would have known how to cheer him. She would have brought the sun to his eyes again. He will travel west like her soon. He is old and it is time."

Adelle touched Shining Water's trembling hand. She knew well the feeling in Shining Water's heart. A tear spilled from the Wendat woman's long black lashes. Adelle stood and went to Yellow Sun. She wrapped his robe tightly around his shoulders and dipped some sagamite, corn soup, into his bowl.

He smiled at her. "You are kind to an old man. That is the way of the People. The strong take care of the weak." He lifted the soup to his shaking lips.

"You are not weak," she told him. "You are Yellow Sun, elder of the Hawk clan." Adelle smiled tenderly.

He coughed again. It was a cough that racked his frail body, and Adelle knew Shining Water was right. Yellow Sun was dying. She wondered at the soul of this kind man, and she recalled her feeling the first night she had arrived in the village. At first she thought it was just her imagination, but it had grown stronger. Darkness. It was her only word to describe it. Darkness shrouded these people and followed them and hung over them even at the happiest of times. The Jesuits once told her that Jesus is the Light of the world, and if one would only come to Him there would be no more darkness. Adelle wished Yellow Sun could see his need for the "whites' " Jesus.

"Have you ever heard the story of the white man's God of Light?" she asked innocently.

He looked at her with a misty far away curiosity. It seemed his thoughts were dim as in a fog, but when he spoke his voice was strong. "When I was a young brave, a white holy man sat by my fire and told me of a Man who was killed by his own people, and He became a god. His blood spilled on the ground to free all men. It is a story not unlike our own." Yellow Sun lowered his bowl with an unsteady hand. "I have not forgotten this story, because this man sacrificed himself for His people such as any Wendat brave would do. The man told me there is great power in His name." Yellow Sun's voice fell away. "Great power," he repeated absentmindedly.

"Have you witnessed this power?" She adjusted the robe that had slipped from his shoulders.

Again Yellow Sun's eyes became cloudy with memories.

Shining Water came and looked into his bowl. "Did the soup warm you, Ayesta?"

Adelle watched silently as they continued in conversation, and then lowered her head to study her hands folded in her lap. Jesus is so much more than a Wendat brave, Yellow Sun, she thought. So much more.

Reynard returned two days before Yellow Sun died. On a cold January morning, Yellow Sun closed his eyes forever.

Reynard had been even more sulky than usual after he returned from Orontony's village, Adelle thought. But the Deer Clan was preparing for Yellow Sun's funeral, and she needed to know what was to be expected of her. The afternoon dragged on. The reality of the tribe's loss seemed too great a burden to be taken in by the senses. Instead, it was measured in small doses and swept over the People as relentless as waves on the shore, no less painful or shocking, but in bites their hearts could digest.

Yellow Sun's relatives wailed loudly and sang their songs of grief. For some it was a complete abandonment to their sorrow which was not looked upon in distaste as it might have been in her own culture, Adelle thought. It was in honor of a man who had served with respect and lived admirably. The entire longhouse was in mourning, and many people had gathered. At last she found a moment alone with Reynard.

"What will happen now?" she whispered, stepping closer to him. Her throat was tight; her voice strained. The emotions in the longhouse floated in the very air, she thought, and she could not stop herself from breathing in their sorrow. She wanted desperately to repel any feeling that attempted to creep in. It was too close to her own loss and too difficult to separate the events.

"The Deer Clan will host a great feast," Reynard explained. "The Feast of the Souls for Yellow Sun. The People will bring food to eat for his friends and family and gifts, clothing, tools." He shrugged. "Whatever they want to honor him. Some will place their gifts inside the grave to help Yellow Sun make a successful journey to the land of the dead. There are various villages in the sky. Someday his spirit will travel the road of souls, toward the setting sun. Until then, it will remain near the village. Until the Feast of the Dead."

Adelle frowned. She did not believe a person would have any need for gifts to help them, and she did not believe in a land of the dead. God would provide for any needs a person might have in their new spirit body. And the land of the dead? A sky village? She believed heaven was the land of the living, the Living God.

She bent over and added another log to the fire. The heat made her skin tingle. Did Yellow Sun now walk amid the flames of hell, or did God pardon ignorant souls? She shivered. The Huron religion was founded in fear, she thought. Christianity was based on love, the love of a Sovereign God for His people, but even love has principles. Sin must be judged. If Yellow Sun had not the covering of a Savior, he too would be judged.

"I cannot do this," she announced.

Reynard watched her blankly, waiting for her to explain.

"Gifts for his journey? The land of the dead? A sky village?" Her voice rose in amazement at these ideas. "These are not things I believe in, Reynard. I cannot participate in a ceremony that does not honor God."

Reynard's dark eyes slowly narrowed; his mouth was set in a thin line. "You will go no matter what you believe," he stated firmly, his anger rising. "You will not disrespect Yellow Sun."

"But–"

"Enough!" he shouted with a wave of his arm.

Adelle glanced nervously in the direction of Shining Water. To her embarrassment, Shining Water had noticed Reynard's furious display, and so did everyone else. Shining Water quickly lowered her eyes, and Adelle turned away. The rebuke seemed to make her shrink even in her own eyes. She slipped behind the deerskin curtain of her sleeping quarters.

Adelle sat on the cold bark floor and wiped away tears of humiliation. There were times she absolutely hated Reynard DuPree, Mighty Fox, whoever he thought he was. She was tired of being forced to do things like a slave, and it was time she told him so. She certainly wasn't going to take any more of his insane fits.

That night Adelle added more wood to the fire and crawled into her sleeping robe. Reynard sat quietly by the fire. He seemed troubled and lost to his thoughts. She figured he was still mad at her. Most likely he was ignoring her, intent on punishing her for having the audacity to have her own mind and not bowing to his command. A flash of new anger shot through her.

"There is something I must tell you," Reynard said quietly.

"What?" Adelle asked not at all pleasantly and rose up on her elbow.

Reynard stared at her for a long minute. "Your mother–"

"My mother died when I was born," she interrupted impatiently.

"Yes." He nodded slowly. "I have known your father all my life. There were other children? Infants, yes?"

Reynard was indifferent to her rudeness. He seemed engrossed in some inner conflict, and Adelle's curiosity was pricked. Even so, Adelle was not about to let go of her grudge easily, and she clung to her anger as a righteous privilege.

"Well then?" she asked defiantly.

Reynard did not waver. He addressed her haughty gaze with his usual air of authority. "When Chaboillier brought me back to Old Coyote, your mother came with him. She picked blue flowers that grew along the river bank to put in her hair. Yellow Sun lived in my father's village then, and he was the only Wendat here who would know the meaning of blue flowers, the name Old Coyote gave your mother."

"You knew my mother?" Adelle blinked in disbelief. "Blue Flowers? You brought me to the one man here who would know I was French by my mother's name?" Reynard's insanity seemed confirmed to her now.

"Yes. It is better to face the enemy with the truth in your hand than to let him stalk you while you plot schemes," Reynard answered. "Yellow Sun understood my debt to your father, and he gave you the safety of his own house."

Adelle lay back down on the platform. She stared at the poles crisscrossing overhead. This should be too amazing to be the truth, she thought. But soon, she closed her eyes as hot tears trickled down her temples and into her hair. She had loved Yellow Sun for Yellow Sun. Never did she realize his abundant kindness to her. God had allowed her Yellow Sun's grace, and tomorrow she had no need to pray Huron prayers; she would have her own. Prayers of thanksgiving to a loving, gentle God who provided for His people when they abandoned all to trust in Him.

"Mighty Fox?" Adelle turned to the fire, but Reynard was gone. Faintly the low, haunting song of sorrow floated in the night air outside. Reynard sang the words of his grief, the loss of his friend, alone in the darkness.

Pierre Antoine licked his lips in anticipation as the Englishman across from him poured more rum into his dingy, dented tin cup.

"I need a certain kind of man– one of cunning and courage." The man rested the rum bottle on the table, calculating his next words. He lifted his own cup to his lips. "It is delicate this work." He winked. "But I think a man of your reputation may find it rather ordinary." He smiled, his thick lips freezing in a grimace over his yellow teeth.

Pierre laughed softly. “Now you have intrigued me, sir. Please go on.”

“Well this business of pelts is fine if you take to it. Yes, it has a certain sense of danger to it, at least at the present, beings we are walking forbidden ground that is. Forbidden by the French rascals anyway.” The man lowered his eyes, suddenly aware of exactly to whom he was speaking. He cleared his throat. “Pardon my rudeness. I-I-”

Pierre nodded knowingly and set his empty cup down. “Go on, please.”

The man filled Pierre’s cup again. “There is talk of war among the tribes.”

“Yes.” Pierre was aware of the British influence that encouraged it.

“Orontony wishes to attack Pontchartrain, and I would appreciate your help in executing the British push to take over the fort.”

Pierre drained his cup. He almost smiled. These British were most competent fellows. He wouldn’t be surprised if they controlled the whole new world some day. “What do you want me to do?” he asked.

Far to the north of Orontony’s village, Jean Baptiste sat among his family at Twisted Bark’s fire. Here the Odawa braves were growing restless, fueling their frigid surroundings with feast after feast to keep the spirit of war fresh. One was in progress, but Jean watched the celebrations with mounting dread. His instinct told him they would have their regrets when this affair was over.

“Hey.” Rising Sky nudged him. “We are talking to you.”

“He does not look like a warrior before a battle does he? More like an anxious old woman,” his brother, Little Thunder, teased.

Red Earth smiled. “A wise, anxious old woman. I am wondering if Orontony, a man who ran from us like a deer before our arrows, deserves to have Odawa men for his braves. In fear he ran from us, and now his words are his only proof of courage.”

"The great chief Macinac has already advised the People, little brother," Standing River reminded him as more of a scold. "Has he not promised to bring the commandant's head to his village, to eat his heart and drink his blood?"

"You have lived too long among the French, Red Earth," Rising Sky scorned his caution. "You are used to their easy ways."

"Perhaps. But it was not ease that I experienced with them three winters ago, my brothers. It was war against the British. It is possible Obwandiyag's words to you are wise. But isn't friendship with the French more tolerable than losing our land to the British? You heard the words spoken at council yourself. The British did not gain their strongholds by keeping their promises. Is it not possible they will make us their slaves as they did the nations of the east? Obwandiyag is braver and mightier than many, but he is not among us. He will oppose Macinac; he will change Macinac's mind. Obwandiyag's war cry is not joined with Orontony, and at this I am thoughtful."

The braves were silent at his words. It was not an angry silence, he observed. They understood the reasoning behind his words. Obwandiyag was a powerful and rising Odawa brave. And even if his brothers differed with his concerns, he would be allowed to make his own decision. This was the reward of respect, one brave to another.

"I will see Orontony for myself, brothers," Jean said. "I want to hear the words he speaks to his people."

Reynard sat long into the cold dark night. Yellow Sun was younger than Old Coyote, and his time of death had come. Soon it would be Old Coyote for whom he sang. These men had accepted him as Wendat, but there were others with a growing hatred for anything white. Would he still be honored?

He pulled the fur robe over his head and closed his eyes. Soon he drifted between sleep and consciousness. Visions passed before his closed eyes. Yellow Sun with Old Coyote. Himself as a young brave at Old Coyote's fire, the smiles, the laughter, the love. And then he saw someone not so clearly, with a full beard and weathered lines at his eyes much like his own. He felt the man's warm hands on his shoulder as he showed him how to aim his musket. He saw the warmth in the man's eyes and how his teeth flashed white against his beard when he smiled. It was a vision that haunted him, shadowed him even now.

He saw himself grown, Mighty Fox, the tried warrior, faithful to his people. Just then a small man came to him through the green forest. A dwarf, Mighty Fox thought, and he frowned, puzzled by the dwarf's strange gestures. He leaned over to hear the man's words, for his lips were moving, but Mighty Fox could hear no sound. The little man drew his war club from behind him and struck Mighty Fox on the head. The green leaves swirled around Mighty Fox, and his knees gave way beneath him.

Reynard awakened with a start. Sweat trickled down his forehead. Was it a dream? All Wendat knew the war spirit appeared in the form of a dwarf. If he came to you and caressed you, all would go well. But if he hit you on the forehead, you must prepare for death. Reynard tossed the robe from his shoulders and shivered as the cold swept over him. He stared numbly into the night. He had just seen the vision foretelling his death.

Reynard DuPree

Revelation

Not long after Yellow Sun's funeral the village prepared for another festival, Ononharoia, or "Upsetting of the Brain." During this ceremony, people burdened by nightmares sought freedom from any repressed desires which they believed were the cause of their torment. The intent was to heal their minds and bodies.

Adelle stepped over the threshold of the longhouse, and a chill breeze ruffled the fur of her robe. Anxiously she gazed into the night sky. It was overcast, and few stars shown overhead. Slowly the drums began their steady pulse, echoing like the devil's footsteps in the forest, she thought. Unfortunately, Reynard had told her how the ceremony would unfold, and she was already wishing it were over. She shivered despite the fires lit in the village. But it wasn't the cold that chilled her.

Reynard came from the longhouse and stopped in front of her. "It is time," he said. "Owa." Come.

Most of the people were already gathered together in the center of the village. To make as much noise as one could seemed to be the goal, and when such a feverish pitch arose that the very hairs on her neck stood on end, Adelle stepped back into the shadows. She watched in growing horror as people began running through the village overturning anything they could. Shrieking loudly, they acted possessed as by some invisible demon. A man ran by her screaming hysterically and nearly knocked her over. These were the people supposedly disturbed by thoughts of longing. But to Adelle the frenzied sight before her was evidence of one thing: complete abandonment of restraint.

She had never been frightened by these Wendat as long as she lived among them. But now, with a feeling close to panic, she hurried back to the safety of her longhouse. She ignored the other families around their fires and was relieved to find her own compartment empty as Shining Water and Running Dog were still outside. She collapsed on the sleeping platform and hugged her knees to her chest in an effort to shut out the horrendous racket all around her. But the din only came closer as it entered the longhouse. Adelle peered cautiously over her knees. The group was just outside her compartment.

"S-s-s-s!" A middle-aged woman with one of her teeth missing and her hair in disarray swayed towards her as if she were a snake. "S-s-s!" she hissed again in Adelle's face and spit on the floor.

Adelle stifled a scream. The woman reached for her, her gnarled fingers just brushing Adelle's shoulder. Then she twisted and danced around the fire as if she had completely lost her mind. Adelle could only watch in paralyzed fear as the woman threw the cooking pots and bowls on the ground, ripped mats and furs from their storage places and tore down the deerskin hanging from the sleeping platform, wailing all the while like some hideously wounded animal.

Soon the troubled group passed through the longhouse, through one end and out the other. Shining Water, smiling happily, returned to her compartment. "You were visited also?" She surveyed the mess around Adelle and began to tidy her own space. "I wonder if I will guess their riddle tomorrow night."

Adelle slid from her seat on the platform and retrieved her pot and bowls. "I hope so," she said. This was one ceremony she didn't want to repeat. The following night the people would come to each fire in the longhouse asking by riddles if the residents could guess the one object their dreams revealed they desired. The resident could guess by giving the dreamer what he thought they were asking for. If he guessed wrong, the dreamer kept the object and continued to the next fire, returning the unwanted object at the end of the ceremony.

Adelle hoped they all got what they wanted. The Wendat believed unfulfilled desires could make them sick, and while Adelle thought this was sometimes true, she wondered what their desires might be. At that moment an even louder uproar began above the screaming, howling dreamers.

Shining Water giggled. "Now what is happening?"

Adelle did not care to know, but she followed her friend back out into the cold night. The roar of flames drowned their shocked gasps. The longhouse next to theirs had caught fire, and flames shot over the tops of the trees. The members of the longhouse fought to put out the fire by slapping the flames with animal skins. They did manage to get the fire under control, but not before it had damaged the longhouse walls.

Surprisingly the fire failed to halt the chaos all around them. It only seemed to fuel the hysteria, Adelle thought. She studied the cheerful faces of the Wendat people standing near her. She had never felt more different from them. She turned back to her own longhouse. Reynard was standing near the door. A curious expression clouded his eyes. Adelle wondered what his thoughts could be. A strange man Papa had said of him, and she agreed. Respected, honored among the People, the kind of honor that bred jealousy in others, and yet for all his fame, he was strangely aloof these days.

The following night the dreamers came back to visit the fires of the turtle clan. They appeared as Adelle had known them before. Two Quills. Leaps-Between-The-Rocks. Little Fawn. Even the crazy old woman who pretended to be a snake was now only Many-Small-Leaves's aunt, Soft Feather. These were the people she had come to love, faults and all. Tonight, without the terrifying screams and play at madness, she could understand their wish for a winter without sickness and death. She could understand their fear, and she so wanted to give them hope.

Finally she realized exactly what separated her from these people who had adopted her as their own. It was not the way they dressed, the way they ate or the way they lived for the most part. It was where they placed their trust. She felt helpless to make them believe in her God, but she could love them with the love He had given her. And indeed, she found she already did. She loved the round-faced little babies, every wrinkle in the aging faces of the old warriors and the way their wives laughed and teased at the cooking fires.

Soft Feather came quietly to Adelle's fire and smiled shyly, her missing tooth the one flaw in her aging beauty. "I have a riddle for Little Turtle," she said. "The chase is over quickly, and my hands are full with its softness."

Adelle grinned, turning to the pile of furs above her. She reached for that certain one, for she knew the answer to Soft Feather's riddle. She pulled down the rabbit fur robe and offered it to Soft Feather.

"A-a-ayee!" shouted Soft Feather, and she ran out of the longhouse.

Adelle laughed and followed her outside where she joined the other villagers as they congratulated Soft Feather by hitting the ground with their fists and shouting, "Hey-ey-ey-ey!"

Winter still had its firm grip on the land when Orontony's council drew near. Reynard gathered his nets and pouches of dried corn and set them on the sleeping platform. "Take everything that is of worth to you," he told Adelle quietly.

Adelle nodded, understanding that he did not intend to return to the village after the council. She wondered what it meant. It was too early for him to be near Pontchartrain. Or was it?

"You must be very careful. Speak to no one," he instructed her. "There is no Yellow Sun in Orontondi's village."

Adelle swallowed hard. She had been thinking that very thing all morning. She dreaded leaving the safety and familiarity of Yellow Sun's village. She would miss Shining Water and the others. She and Reynard were going to the council merely as spectators since the clan chiefs and war chiefs would be the ones doing the bulk of the speaking. Even so, many of the Wendat would attend just for the privilege of hearing for themselves the words of their representatives. As clan chief, Old Coyote would be there too, as well as the chiefs from all other Wendat villages. It would be a large gathering of Wendat leaders, one that would decide the fate of the French.

Obediently, Adelle carried her pack to the canoe and climbed in. She readied her paddle as Reynard pushed out, guiding their canoe to join the others already in the water. Silently, smoothly, Brave Arrow glided past, his eyes fixed sternly on Reynard. Adelle held her paddle blade still against the current to let him pass, glancing discretely over her shoulder at Reynard. He didn't seem to notice Brave Arrow's venomous warning.

Adelle paddled many miles until the faint sound of drums became louder. She grew weak at the thought of stepping foot in Orontony's village. God has brought me here, she reminded herself. It was the one thing she believed without doubt now. She had come on this journey for a purpose. Only God had yet to reveal what it was.

With the cold wind numbing her cheeks, she dipped her paddle in the water in perfect rhythm with Reynard. Swiftly their canoe cut through the water behind the others. The bright sun glittered down gaily on the sparkling white snow as if it knew nothing of the sinister intent of the warriors below. Soon the path to Orontony's village could be seen from the protected waters of the southern shore. Canoes littered the shoreline where the drums beat a somber welcome as they pulled to shore. After beaching their canoes, they followed the path through the village walls.

Adelle gripped her pack until her knuckles were white. She pressed it close to her in an attempt to quiet her thumping heart. But the drums were deafening now; their pounding vibrated in her chest. Reynard walked ahead with the men, but she soon lost sight of him in the throng of Indians. Representatives from the Saulters, Pouteaouatami, Nadowessioux, Shawnee, Outawae, Miamis and other smaller tribes clustered inside the village.

Forcing her expression into a mask of indifference, Adelle waited with the other women until one of their hosts led them to an extra longhouse built for visitors. Adelle was offered quarters in a smaller longhouse with only two compartments. For this she was thankful, since she had planned to keep to herself as much as possible.

Late in the afternoon, the Wendats prepared for the evening feast. A huge fire was lit in the middle of the village. Dancing, singing, feasting and storytelling lasted well into the night. Adelle sat quietly among the Indians. Not even Orontony himself could have known by her appearance and behavior that an enemy sat in their midst, she played her part so well.

It was almost dawn when Adelle and Reynard returned to the small longhouse. To her dismay they were not alone. A young brave sat near his fire in the other compartment. His black hair was long, below his shoulders, and sectioned in half by a middle part from his forehead to his nape. Each section was gathered together, the lengths wrapped with a dyed red ribbon that spiraled around until it reached the bottom. Here it was wound about the hair and tied to keep it in place.

Two feathers were attached at the back of his crown, the tips pointing downward instead of erect like most Wendat. Red dye was drawn in a broad line over his cheeks and nose. Finer grey lines stretched from the center of his lower lip to the center tip of his chin. A crude drawing of a wolf was tattooed on his chest.

Adelle recognized the style as that of the Outawae. With a sinking heart, she realized the scope of Orontony's influence. She had seen this type of tattoo before near L' Arbre Croche more than sixty leagues overland to the north of Pontchartrain. He did not appear to have a family or any comrades staying with him. He nodded solemnly when Reynard passed and politely turned his back to offer them privacy. Adelle thought this odd. Most Indians held no regard for one's seclusion.

The following day, the council began in earnest. Adelle sat cross-legged near the outer edge of the circle of Indians. At first they gathered in their own clans to talk. After this, they gathered as a nation. Speaker after speaker stood to state the reason for the council, to say his piece and to repeat the speaker's words before him. If what was spoken was agreeable, a hearty, "Haa-uh!" was shouted. The louder the shout, the greater the agreement.

Finally Orontony took his turn. Adelle strained to see this infamous warrior chief. He looked disappointingly as any other Wendat, not as muscular as Old Coyote even. His speech, however, was the best of any chief yet. He chose to express himself through long, vivid stories. So lengthy, Adelle found herself losing interest in them. It was enough to say his words were full of hostility toward the French, Adelle thought. But he emphasized the good of all the people of every tribe. Hatred was deemed patriotic, actually encouraged by the affirming nods of the British who sat facing the crowd. The Indians hung on Orontony's every word; the haa-uh's resounding mightily from every side.

Each chief spoke again as well as anyone else who had anything to say. So it was no surprise the council went on for days until all had exhausted their opinions and the clans had reached a consensus: all French in Pontchartrain and the lake posts would be killed.

The feasting continued as the war chiefs plotted their schemes of death. Adelle noticed Reynard had been strangely silent throughout the council. But she gave him little thought as she was absorbed with concern for her countrymen. The traders Papa had known all his life were in danger, and they had no idea to what extent. The posts perched along the shores of the Erie, or Okswego, the Bay and the rivers inland, were occupied by men trying to make a living. All were in danger. She felt sick.

And so the plans were made. Adelle listened carefully and began to understand why Orontony was so respected. His cunning equaled no other Indian she had ever met. He seemed to know the French as well as his own people, a predator who knew his prey so well, his victory was assured. One could almost imagine Satan's serpent tongue in Orontony's ear, his words were so fully cunning and evil at the same time. The British were present, of course. Oh, how she hated their yellow smiles, she thought bitterly.

At last it was done. The Miamis and Wendat were to wipe out every French in the Maumee country. The Fox and Pouteaouatami were given Green Bay and the Bois Blanc Islands. Not one white was to be spared; not one mercy to be granted. Adelle felt the force of this declaration.

For himself, Orontony chose Pontchartrain. It was decided certain Wendats near there would sleep inside the fort in French homes. This would be no cause for alarm since it was commonly done anyway. But this time, the Wendats must murder the people in whose house they slept. Orontony set the date, a holy day during Pentecost. Nothing would seem amiss, for the focus would be on their white religion and the pitied savages under their roof. Adelle shuddered at the simplicity of it all.

The council drew to a close. The final feast was prepared. There was a heightened sense of glee in the air, for the prospect of bloodshed appeared to animate the warriors. But amid all this, Adelle sat numbly on the cold ground as the people around her trickled toward the pots of steaming food. Many had been drinking already. They were the ones stumbling about as the crowd dispersed around the council fire. The other side of the small clearing was visible now, and she could see Reynard standing with Old Coyote.

Old Coyote, indeed. A perfect name for a grizzled, graying old man who never smiled. She wanted to hate them, every stinking one of them.

She shook her head, blinking back tears. "God, You must do something to stop them." She mouthed the words. For truly, if she gave sound to her voice, she would curse them all.

She rose slowly, knowing she must act her part. But she lagged behind the others, engrossed in her troubles, and so it was by accident she caught Reynard watching her. Quickly he averted his gaze, but not before Adelle read the sentiment in his expression. He was worried. Adelle bit her lip. Perhaps he would not be able to keep her safe, even if he were the son of Old Coyote.

Reynard stood beside Old Coyote, his mother's brother, the man who had raised him as his oldest son. He longed for Old Coyote to soothe his fears and give him wisdom as he had done when he was a boy. This growing unrest in his soul disturbed him, and for once he did not know the way to peace.

"Ayesta," Reynard said when they were alone. "I am troubled that my heart does not rejoice with my brothers. I hear the words spoken, and they do not bring me confidence. You have walked long on the earth, why is this so?"

Old Coyote turned to Reynard, searching his face for some time. "You are strong for the People, my son. You have proved your loyalty to your Wendat brothers. Do not fear the stirring in your soul. It is right to question the act of war, for a warrior must not die foolishly without purpose, and your heart is testing the words spoken against this truth. It is your eiachia and yandiyonra.

Your emotion and your intellect struggling for control." Old Coyote placed his wrinkled hand against Reynard's chest.

"Orontondi speaks bold words, my son," he continued. "Words that not all the Wendat agree upon. Look, do you see Big Turtle, or Gray Claw?" He gestured. "They do not trust the Iroquois, our old enemy. They believe the Iroquois will one day fight with the British against us so they are not here. And there are others who do not wish to follow Orontondi into battle, plunder or no plunder. Your yandiyonra sees these things; it questions you to test you. But war councils belong in the house of cut off heads, otinontsiskiaj ondaon. To be ready for battle, the eiachia must control you. Seek for wisdom, my son."

Reynard nodded. He would do this. Old Coyote turned to the festival, and they both took their place among the Wendat.

Adelle sighed. She did not wish to join the feast, but this would be expected, so she made her way through the din of drums and whoops to the bonfire. Two Englishmen stood near Orontony. One shook his hand; the other took a swig from the bottle he carried. Adelle stopped. She sensed something vaguely familiar about the one with the bottle. Impossible. And yet... The man turned his back and disappeared into the crowd. Adelle raised her eyebrows. How silly. She did not even know any British, and she did not care to.

Two days later most of the visitors left. Reynard had lingered one more day to see Old Coyote off, so they were the only Wendat that remained from Yellow Sun's village. Adelle had expected to leave with Old Coyote that afternoon, but Reynard still sat with the elders in Orontony's village. She was impatient to leave this place. That night they sat alone in the small longhouse, for the Outawae brave, though not gone from the village, had not slept there the past two nights.

Adelle unfolded the sleeping robe on the bunk. "Why aren't we leaving, Reynard? Why are you here?"

Reynard glanced at her, but he said nothing. He was stripped to the waist and smoking his pipe. At regular intervals he blew smoke into the fire and fanned the smoke over his skin. Adelle waited for him to finish. She knew he was praying and offering tobacco, probably to some war spirit. With an impatient sigh she slumped on the sleeping platform, growing more disgusted the longer she watched him. Surely, his real father was lost to him, she thought. Finally, Reynard set his pipe aside.

"Do you not fear God?" Adelle reproached him.

"I fear no one," he replied. "My enemies fear me." He folded his hands in his lap and stared into the yellow leaping flames.

"Then you are a foolish man, Reynard DuPree!" Adelle fairly spat the words out in contempt. "You give yourself to the shifting sands of this world when all that is important is what is eternal."

But her opinion seemed to avail little. His face showed the emotion of a flat gray stone.

"My father once told me not to spend myself for what has no worth," she continued, somewhat irked by his indifference to her criticism. " 'But how will I know what is worthy?' I asked him. And he said this, 'You will know if it is true and lasting.' Is this world, this country, who has what, lasting, Reynard? Or is birth a cycle unto death, and then we live what is true?"

Reynard turned again to the fire, and his continuing silence ignited her anger.

"What survives the burning fire of judgment, Reynard? Orontony? The People?" Adelle laughed bitterly. "I think not. Are you ready to die a Wendat? Die like the spiritual dog you are? Do you remember your father at all, or have you prostituted yourself completely to the Wendat way?"

Reynard hit the floor with his fist. "Enough!" he shouted knocking aside his pipe as he stood. His bare chest heaved, and his nostrils flared. "You will speak no more!"

Adelle was stunned by his reaction when it finally came, yet at that moment a conviction formed in her that was so clear, so true and so real it seemed to settle into her spirit like a rod of iron. There was no audible sound as it chinked into place, but its force stiffened the matter that molded her flesh, giving her a strength that was not her own. Suddenly, she realized the purpose for which she had come. It had been with her all along, but she had resented it, even hated it. It was Reynard. God desired Reynard for Himself.

Bold confidence replaced her fear. "It is not enough!" she shouted back. She rose to meet his fierce glare. "I know that you have knowledge of God. That you have heard of the Christ, but you reject Him. Now He is giving you another chance, Reynard. Don't turn your back on Him like you have your earthly father!"

Reynard towered over her. His eyes were cold malicious slits, and the muscles in his cheeks flinched with rage. Adelle braced herself as he took a step toward her. He was close enough that she could smell the sunflower oil on his skin and feel his tobacco breath on her face. She knew he was going to hit her, but this was the time the Lord had prepared her for. She stood firmly, raising her chin in defiance.

"The devil controls you, Reynard," she said. "But I am not afraid of him. I am not afraid."

Reynard blinked. He stepped back, looking as surprised as Adelle felt. Angrily he turned away, grabbing a log to stir the fire. He dropped to his knees next to the glowing embers and kept his back to her. Adelle sank onto the platform again. She closed her eyes, clutching her hands together to keep them from shaking. She did not think she would ever forget the hatred in his appearance. It was as if she had just faced evil itself, but it had shrunk back, powerless to overtake her. In the morning, Reynard was gone.

Anxiously, Jean Baptiste waited for DeLongueuil's messenger at a designated place far inland from Orontony's village, beyond the fork in the river and the Wendat trails. The commandant would be happy to learn he had the loyalty of the Odawa tribes near Pontchartrain at least. But how long must he wait, Jean fretted. Orontony's council was over. Soon tribes would be filling the forest on their way home, then it would no longer be safe for a meeting with Frenchmen. He lingered for two days. Something must have happened because his contact should have met him by now. He decided to return to the village for the time being. He would have one more opportunity for a rendezvous before he must leave to warn DeLongueuil himself if necessary.

He had almost reached the fork in the river when a line of menacing gray clouds appeared overhead. The breeze became gusts, swaying the bare limbs of the forest overhead and pushing the smaller trees to and fro against their brothers rooted beside them. The trees moaned under the strain, their limbs crying out with painful creaks. Jean had to steady his fur hat or it would have been torn away by the increasingly fierce blasts. The storm was approaching quickly. A big one, he thought as he inspected the clouds again.

If he had followed the superstitions of his faith, he might have been apprehensive about his union with the French government and his missing contact in light of the approaching storm. It would be an omen of evil. The Odawa believed evil spirits could bring troubles upon them. And surely God never brought troubles upon the righteous. Therefore he had strayed from the right path somewhere. But, Jean thought as he looked up at the sky, it was winter, and storms were to be expected.

Far into the forest, the wind howled through the trees. Reynard covered his snare with snow and sat back on his haunches. Dense clouds spread across the sky. A storm was coming in quickly. He picked up the two dead beavers he had just caught and clambered up a steep hill. Snow was already falling when he reached a natural depression in the rock much like a hollowed out bowl laid on its side. He tossed the beavers on the floor of the small cave and set to gathering some wood for a fire. He would wait out the storm.

The fire crackled beside him as he cut off the hind legs of the beaver then sliced a clean line around the legs, tail and straight down the center of the belly from the jaw to the vent. He loosened the skin, carefully cutting it free, making as few cuts as possible. After spreading it out to dry, he cut some of the meat off the carcass and roasted it over the fire.

Adelle may worry if he did not make it back by nightfall, he thought. "Hmph!" he grunted angrily. She had a tongue of fire, but the courage of a warrior. Last night her words had gripped him like never before. Shifting sands. That is what this country was becoming, shifting under the weight of British lies and desperate men bent on the quest for land.

Revenge was honorable, necessary for a warrior. Orontondi wanted revenge against the French. Why then did he hesitate at the words of this powerful chief? He had never questioned before, but now...

Orontondi did not seem powerful, only a British pawn. Reynard did not want to stand alongside these British dogs. This thought surprised him. Months ago, he would have followed Orontondi into battle and would have been honored to fight with him. What had happened? Did he now have the heart of a woman?

He had been so sure of his mission that night on the Rivière aux Raisias. The certainty tempted him to think it was a gift from the Creator. A young woman who could read and not just any woman, Chaboillier's daughter.

Chaboillier loved her deeply it was clear. This he could use to his advantage. The old man might not have liked it, but in exchange for his silence, Reynard would take her with him and guarantee her safety. His too if he wanted it. If he didn't keep his end of the bargain, the young girl would die. If he didn't agree to the arrangement, they would both die anyway. But the certainty had vanished. He also realized, he would have never allowed her to be harmed.

The wet snow fell in a blinding sheet of white. Reynard skinned the other beaver and cooked the meat. It was good this time alone. He must try to understand these things. He reached for his pipe, but his belt was empty. Then he remembered where he had dropped it by the fire last night.

Do you remember your father? she had asked. Her words angered him even now. He saw Adelle, her smooth skin and doe-like eyes. His anger melted before her image like the snow near his fire. She was so young, like a spring fawn in a forest of wolves, young enough to be his own daughter. She hated him; that was her right, but he must keep her safe for Chaboillier, for himself.

The afternoon faded into early evening, and the sky was darkening in the village. Frantically Adelle ripped open the canoe pack. Had Reynard left for good? She had not seen him all day. She thought nothing out of the ordinary when Reynard hadn't eaten the morning meal with her, and she had been gathering wood with the other women since then. She dug into the supply of corn. Not even a handful was missing, but that meant little. He was capable of fending for himself. She tossed the pack on the bunk. Her words had held some truth, but...

"Oh, why did I let my anger speak for me?" she said aloud, knowing her words had not been fair.

If Reynard had left her here alone, perhaps she deserved it, she thought. Then she saw his pipe. It still lay where he had left it by the now smoldering fire. Adelle breathed a sigh of relief and sank to the bark covered floor. Shakily she reached under the platform. His nets were gone. He had left to set his traps along the river. But the fact that his pipe lay on the floor forgotten told her something more. It was part of his oki, and he would never have left it behind.

Something troubled him. Suddenly she was sorry for every hateful word she had ever spoken to him. Truly, she never would have made it to Pontchartrain alone unharmed. He had brought her to the Wendat for her safety. He had kept his word to her, and faithful to his promise, he had demanded nothing of her. She would not have fared so well in the hands of even a French trader. He had risked his safety for hers, and when he had lost in death a beloved friend, she offered no sympathy and never any words of gratitude for his kindness.

Adelle bit her lip. Reynard was a hard man; she did not understand his ways. But she knew this: God had brought to her the one man in all of New France who felt any responsibility toward her at all. His friendship was genuine, and it had lasted through all of her childish tantrums. Adelle smiled through her tears.

"He is worthy, Papa," she whispered. "Reynard DuPree is worthy."

Her shoulders shook in silent sobs. "Ho-ma-yen-de-zuit-et-et-rang. Father God, forgive me. I have sinned against You, against the blessing You have provided. I have judged him harshly." Her voice trailed away; she realized the cost of her sin. She must go to Reynard and ask for his forgiveness.

She stood, wiping her eyes on her sleeve. She held the flap of deerskin aside and stepped out into the cold. A bitter wind tore through the village despite the high walls, lifting the fallen snow and hurling it against the longhouses. Low gray clouds hovered overhead, blotting out the sun. She trudged through the village, bent forward at the waist so fierce was the growing wind. Few people were out. A young woman carrying a basket of corn from the storehouse struggled against the gale. Adelle stopped her.

"Have you seen Mighty Fox? He went to set traps." Adelle hoped for an answer, but the girl only shook her head.

The wind was like ice on Adelle's skin. She had no choice but to return to the longhouse and wait. The wind pushed her all the way back. A heavy, wet snow fell as she stood looking over the village one last time before entering the longhouse. She added more wood to her fire and brushed the snow from her fur robe. She hoped Reynard would make it back soon.

The next morning, Reynard had not returned. Adelle closed the deerskin flap and absently stirred the corn soup. The snow had fallen to a depth just below her knee, but the drifts were deeper. She and her father had been stranded by storms such as this one. They came in quickly across the lakes.

Morning passed. The snow fell lightly now, but the bitter wind still tore at the deerskin covering the entrance. Adelle strapped bear paw snowshoes over her moccasins and pulled on a beaver robe. She must find Reynard. She must make things right between them. She could wait no longer.

No one gave Adelle a second glance as she trekked through the village and into the forest beyond. The lighter snow swirled in great puffs across the blue-white crust dumped the night before. Her breath escaped in misty clouds that froze in droplets on the edges of her furry hood. Reynard would set his nets where the beaver were abundant near the inner wooded streams. She did not know this country, but she had seen the mouth of the Saundustee when they arrived, and she followed it inland. It was mostly snow covered, but patches of inky blue flowed openly in places.

She travelled a great distance from the village before she found one of Reynard's snare traps with a beaver already in it. Soon the forest opened into a large clearing. The sun's light upon her was warmer here, and she sat down to rest. She drew out her pouch of dried corn tied to her waist. She ate to satisfy the emptiness in her stomach and moved on.

At the other end of the clearing, beyond the bend in the river, the waters seemed to fork, since two paths divided the trees on either side. No smoke was visible to indicate a fire, and a closer look revealed no tracks. She hated to give up, but it was getting late.

Adelle turned back, her own tracks already erased by the wind. As she neared the middle of the clearing, she suddenly realized she did not know from which direction she had come. She took a few steps down the slope of a large drift.

"And I told Papa I was as able as any Anishinabekwe," she chastised herself. Cutting across a low depression, she searched for anything familiar, a twisted limb, the rise of the earth, but the storm had draped everything in a monotonous blanket of white. She squinted into the sun, trying to calculate its position in the sky.

"That is west," she decided. "The village is this way." She turned to her left. A soft swishing sound caught her attention. No wind blew now. No branch brushed another. She listened closely, instantly cautious. A ridge flanked her on both sides and she could not see beyond it. The sound came again. Puzzled, she looked down at her feet. Water! She must be standing on a thin covering of ice!

A crack sounded to her right. She rushed forward, lunging for the ridge she now knew was the bank of a large pond. But it was too late. The snow beneath her fell away as the thin ice caved inward. She dropped into the icy water, her screams piercing the frigid air. Her heavy robe and snowshoes were like weights. She struggled to free herself, but the effort proved too great to be accomplished. Wildly she groped the ice with one hand as the strong current feeding the main river threatened to sweep her away. She was pulled under once, twice; she lost count.

I am going to die, she thought as she surfaced again, gasping for breath.

The cold air pained her lungs. Her robe clung to her and drew her down. "Jesus, help me!" she sobbed.

The cold water quickly stole her strength, and she reached out knowing it would be her last time. Her fingers touched something hard. She could barely see; her eyelids were already growing stiff with cold.

A root! She wrapped her fingers around it and pulled. A surge of power coursed through her arms as she pulled herself up and out. She rolled away, the river gurgling its ominous warning behind her. Shivering, Adelle collapsed on the snow. Swoosh, swoosh, swoosh. Not again, Adelle thought. She tried to get up, for she feared she was falling through again. She fought the blackness that threatened to overtake her, stubbornly willing her eyes open.

Snow fell softly on her forehead. Snowshoes. Her eyelids drooped and blinked open. A brown face. A kind face. A warm hand.

I must be dreaming, she thought, and wearily surrendered to the darkness.

Death to the Indian

Warmth. Delicious, comforting, satisfying warmth. It blanketed her. It surrounded her. It filled the very air. Adelle opened her eyes. The fire popped and hissed next to her. A steaming pot hung over its flames. She drew her hands from underneath the bearskin covering her.

"She is awake."

She heard Reynard's voice and turned her head toward the sound. He was sitting beside her. Slowly she recognized the small longhouse compartment and realized she was lying on a pile of furs. A young brave, not Running Dog, no, certainly not Running Dog, came and knelt beside Reynard. Adelle frowned, trying to focus. She felt so fuzzy. This man was not Wendat.

"This is Red Earth Runner," Reynard told her. "He has saved your life. You fell through the ice. Do you remember?"

Adelle frowned again and nodded. She recognized him now as the Outawae brave staying in the next compartment.

"He heard your screams."

Adelle raised up on her elbows. A tightness in her chest shortened her breath. She felt so tired.

Reynard gently pushed her back down. "You must rest. You have been asleep many, many days. Do what Red Earth tells you, and you will become strong again. He is a healer."

Adelle reached for Reynard's hand. "Do not leave me," she whispered. It was all she could say, she felt so weak.

Reynard squeezed her hand. "I am Mighty Fox, son of Old Coyote."

Adelle tried to smile, but the blackness overtook her again.

Reynard clenched his teeth. Slowly he let go of her hand and drew the fur over her arms. She lay there so frail and ashen. Gingerly, he touched her cheek as if he were afraid he might awaken her. He could not say what he felt. That she was more brave and more beautiful than any Wendat woman he had ever met. That he had come to love her, not as a man loves a woman but as a father loves a daughter, and that he would protect her with his own life. No, he would never say these things to her; she would not understand.

It was no coincidence their lives had come together this way, he thought. What began as a selfish scheme to please his Wendat brothers resulted in binding him to the one person alive who could stir any loyalty to his French past. The whiteness of her skin chilled him. Truly, the day was coming when the color of their skin could cost them both their lives.

His emotions troubled him, and he grabbed Red Earth by the arm. "Nothing must happen to her," he snapped. "Nothing!"

Long into the night Jean Baptiste sat with Mighty Fox, the respected Wendat warrior. It had unnerved him at first when he discovered this was the man with whom he shared a longhouse. His Odawa friends had long since departed and he had agreed to stay behind at DeLongueuil's request forwarded by the delinquent messenger– a decision he immediately regretted. But Orontony seemed eager to begin a campaign. Perhaps, Jean thought, he could persuade the braves against any rash action until word reached Pontchartrain. He would have one more chance to inform DeLongueuil by the trade route his messengers were told to use before his time here would be over. In the meantime, he would be passing his days with a savvy Wendat whose young wife he had just rescued from certain death– a situation that proved most providential as the man had befriended him.

Strange this pair, though. For days she had babbled deliriously in French, a good part of which were prayers of the Jesuits. And who was Pierre? Mighty Fox explained nothing, but he seemed nervous. Perhaps "Red Earth" was not the only one with secrets, Jean thought.

Mighty Fox passed him his pipe. "It is Wendat custom to invite the curers," he said. "I do this not to insult you my friend, but to honor my People. They wish to help me, to heal my wife."

Jean Baptiste nodded, exhaling the smoke. He wondered if Little Turtle would be as grateful. She seemed to be a Christian Wendat. He watched Mighty Fox closely. "She will welcome their prayers then," he said as more of a question than a statement.

Mighty Fox took the pipe again. "She will welcome their concern." He tried unsuccessfully to hide the irritation in his voice.

Jean Baptiste hid a smile. The old fox, waagosh, had said everything without admitting anything. He was wise, this one. "Tell me of your curers," he said, reaching for the pipe.

"There is the Dance of Fire," Mighty Fox said a bit wearily. "But, Awataerohi is the ceremony they use most. Curers will hold hot coals in their hands then place their warmed hands on her. Others will put hot stones in their mouths and speak the spirits' power into her ear. Others may blow pieces of hot coal or ashes at her." Mighty Fox's voice trailed away. He passed the pipe to the young brave.

"I feel as an old man," he said. "I am tired. Forgive me."

Red Earth took a last draw on the pipe and got up. "In the morning," he said.

"In the morning," Mighty Fox repeated, reaching for his pipe again. He knelt next to Little Turtle.

Jean Baptiste withdrew to his own compartment across the aisle and pretended to be asleep. But he watched Mighty Fox through half closed lids, for his curiosity only grew the more he talked to this man. He liked his reserved manner and slow deliberate speech. He was a man who weighed his words, and Jean admired that. So many men spoke quickly, revealing all the pent up ignorance in their foolish hearts. But this man was wise. One he could learn from.

Mighty Fox knelt by Little Turtle a long time. She was beautiful, Jean thought. It surprised him that the more time he spent near her, the more he envied Mighty Fox. He tried to push these thoughts away, but they continued to assault his best intentions.

Presently Mighty Fox drew papers from his jacket. Jean blinked. Was he seeing what he thought he was seeing? Mighty Fox reached under the bunk and appeared to be digging under the bark floor. Having accomplished his task, he slid a box crafted out of woven reeds toward him that apparently was buried under the sleeping platform for safekeeping. Placing the papers into it, he then laid his shirt aside and sat before the fire staring into the flickering light. He picked up the box, turning it over a few times as if deciding what to do with it.

Why would a Wendat warrior keep papers, Jean asked himself. Letters? For what purpose? To trade? As oki? He didn't know very many Indians who could read. Questions. Questions that kept him awake and made his curiosity burn ever more intensely. He must find out what those letters said. Their contents may be important to the forts.

He waited hours until Mighty Fox lay down, and he could hear his even breathing. Stealthily he crept beside Mighty Fox. He dared not even breathe. Mighty Fox was no fool, and he would have no explanations if he were discovered.

"God help me," he prayed silently. Deftly he lifted the box and slid the letters out. He unfolded them slowly, his eyes on the sleeping Mighty Fox. He scanned the letters quickly. Most were in English, but he could recognize names, and one contained French phrases with reports of Nicholas's conspiracy against the French. In essence, the British in Sandoski were doing their part to see that Orontony followed through on his planned attack against Pontchartrain. They were especially enthusiastic about a certain addition to their ranks, "a most fortunate convert who would greatly advance their cause by knowing all things French."

Jean replaced the letters into the box and silently returned to his own compartment. He lay down on his bunk and stared at the beams overhead. A convert who would know all things French. A Frenchman who had gone over to the British side? An informant who would be giving them intimate details? Would this be a trader? But what could a French trader desire more than his drink and his women? He doubted a trader would make the effort.

A soldier then. There weren't many others in Pontchartrain, he conceded. Either could be bribed. It was frustrating this puzzle. But a soldier? Jean shook his head. A soldier may have the intellect, but surely it would be impossible that a man who fought for his country would then desert it in such treachery. And what of Mighty Fox? Exactly what did he plan to do with these letters? He yawned. It would have to wait until morning.

Adelle slowly opened her eyes. The fire blazed beside her, and the steaming pot still hung over it. She looked around, but Mighty Fox was no where to be seen.

"Mighty Fox?" she called, her parched throat, stretching with the effort.

Red Earth came from across the aisle and knelt beside her. "Drink this," he told her, holding a wooden spoon to her lips.

Adelle tasted the warm broth. "Mighty Fox–"

"He will come soon," Red Earth interrupted. He filled the spoon again and offered it to her. His eyes watched her steadily.

Curiously, she returned his gaze. "Thank you," she barely whispered. She remembered his eyes. Soft and kind.

He guided another spoonful toward her. "You must sit up now," he said after she had swallowed. "If you do not, you will become too weak." He laid aside the spoon and bent over her. He smelled like green grass warmed by the sun.

His arms were strong; he lifted her easily, and Adelle was shocked she did indeed need his strength for her own was greatly wanting. She studied his gentle face. The warrior paint was gone, and his skin was clear and tanned. The room began to swirl, and she closed her eyes. Slowly she opened them again.

"Do you remember me?" he asked, handing her a bowl of the broth.

His voice was soft and deep, the kind that one never tires of listening to, Adelle thought. She nodded, swallowing the warm liquid.

"Do you remember waking up before?"

Adelle thought for a moment. "Yes."

"You have been asleep many, many more days since then. Coughing." He tapped his chest. "I am a-a-" He stumbled over the right Wendat word. "Mshkikiinni," he finished in Outawae, holding up a small pouch. "Peppermint, elder flower, gumweed, black cherry bark, these have helped to heal you."

Adelle smelled the herbs in the steaming pot and was aware of the grease smeared on her skin. She smiled. "I am grateful for your kindness."

Red Earth smiled boyishly. His teeth were white and evenly spaced. "My grandmother was a mshkikiinni; that is Odawa for doctor."

Adelle nodded. She was familiar with the Outawae language. But of course, Red Earth did not know this. "Do you live here in the village?" She glanced at his tattoo which marked him as a member of the wolf clan.

"No," Red Earth replied. "I will leave soon."

"Where is Mighty Fox?"

"He went to gather his traps. The best of the season has passed."

"Passed?" Adelle frowned.

"Yes. It is the time of the new grass. Mnookmig."

Spring? She had been sick for weeks!

Red Earth saw her surprise. "You do not remember? You were awake some of the time."

Adelle frowned. "Just nightmares," she said finally.

Red Earth did not seem to understand.

"I dreamed of people crawling around in animal skins," she laughed weakly. "I think they were breathing fire."

He smiled. "That was the healing ceremony."

"Oh," Adelle shrugged. She was glad she was not awake.

"You are familiar with the ceremony?" Red Earth asked innocently and filled the bowl again.

Adelle lifted the bowl to her lips. The broth was good, and the more she ate the stronger she felt. "Um, yes." She had heard of it once while at Yellow Sun's village.

She stopped abruptly. The council. If it were spring, the attack on Pontchartrain was fast approaching. She glanced at Red Earth and back into her bowl.

She was aware that he was studying her. "Your broth is good," she told him. "I feel stronger."

"Then you must stand and walk. Quickly you will be new again." Red Earth reached for the bowl.

As he took the bowl his hand brushed hers, and Adelle was surprised by the tenderness in his touch.

He smiled. "Come." He jerked his head and held out his hand.

She reached for his hand, and he pulled her to her feet. She held onto him in an effort to steady herself. The room seemed to swim for a minute before she got her bearings. Bravely, she took a few awkward steps around the compartment then slumped onto the bunk again.

Red Earth laughed. "So Little Turtle is back among the living ones!"

He held her hand lightly, and Adelle was comforted by his warmth.

"You are like the wobbly, little fawn who soon will run and leap with the others," he said.

She smiled up at him. He was older than she and very different in manner from any man she knew. Behind Red Earth the deerskin was pulled aside, and Mighty Fox stopped at the threshold.

"Mighty Fox!" Adelle cried out with a big smile.

Red Earth turned. When he saw Mighty Fox he released her hand and backed away.

Joy rose in her, but Reynard did not return her greeting. He looked first to Red Earth. Slowly he crossed the room, his eye on the young man. Reynard knelt in front of her. "It is good," he said of her renewed health. Then he smiled, and she knew he meant it.

Tears filled her eyes. Quickly she brushed them away. "I was afraid–" she began, but Reynard held up his hand. She knew she needed to be careful of her words.

He turned to Red Earth. Without a sound, Red Earth disappeared behind the buckskin door, and they were alone.

"Why were you so far from the village?" Reynard asked her.

"I came looking for you." Adelle blinked away more tears.

"I told you I would bring you safely to Pontchartrain, Adelle. You must trust me–"

"No, you misunderstand," Adelle interrupted. "At first I feared that you left me here, but then I found your pipe, and I wanted–" Adelle steadied her trembling lip. "I wanted to tell you that I was sorry."

Reynard blinked, and the muscles in his cheek flinched when he clenched his jaw.

"I am grateful for your kindness to me, Reynard, and I am sorry I have acted badly toward you."

Reynard placed his warm, rough hand over hers. "You must get well, Adelle. We must leave soon. It is spring and–"

"I want to stay with you, Reynard," she interrupted again. "I've changed my mind. I- I do not really know anyone in Pontchartrain. Well, Pierre, but he may have left by now."

"Pierre?" Reynard asked as if he had heard the name before.

"Yes, Pierre Antoine. He was a soldier I met in Fort St. Joseph, but I have not known him long, and Papa..." Adelle gave Reynard a wry smile. She was embarrassed to reveal her youthful secret. "Papa did not like him; he thought Pierre dishonest." She stared into her lap. Talking of these old stray threads did not create the anxiety they had when Papa was alive, when the prospect of love was new.

She felt no stirring at the mention of Pierre's name like she had a few months ago. But, she realized with regret, her world was vastly different a few months ago, and at this moment her priorities were different as well.

"You want to marry this man?"

Adelle brought her attention back to Reynard. He genuinely seemed interested. "Well, I had thought of it at first." Adelle laughed weakly. She suddenly felt foolish.

"Now?" Reynard demanded.

"To be honest, I have not thought of him," she answered.

Reynard remained quiet for some time, looking once to the empty compartment across from theirs. Adelle was sensitive enough to his moods by now that she knew it was best to keep still.

All at once he stood up. "Eat," he commanded and gave her another bowl of broth.

"Can I stay with you?" Adelle pleaded, obediently sipping the broth.

"No," he replied curtly. "Whatever happens, you must return to the French. I have nothing to offer you."

"But–"

"No more words, Adelle. Eat."

Adelle felt like crying, but she sighed and drank the soup.

Outside, Jean Baptiste crouched alongside the longhouse as if he were busy lashing a loose pole. If he strained, he could faintly make out the voices inside. Adelle and Reynard were not Wendat names. And Pierre Antoine. He had heard that name before, but where? He was leaving in three days. Perhaps he could learn more by then.

Reynard filled Adelle's bowl again. Orontondi had grown restless these last months, and the war chiefs were anxious to begin something–anything. For reasons that still bothered him, he had no desire to join with these braves. His friends were growing curious at his silence. Now that Adelle's condition had improved, it was time to leave for Old Coyote's village, the sooner the better.

He placed a log on the fire to keep the soup in the kettle warm. But he opened the flap over the door to let in fresh air. The temperature was mild, and the breeze freshened the smoke-stale air. Adelle sat quietly on the platform drinking her soup. Reynard absently stirred the fire. He should say something to her, he thought.

"It is good that you like the Wendat," he said, staring into the kettle. "That you have come to trust me. I am... pleased. But you belong with the French. You are tired now and weak. You cling to what is familiar, but later you will long for your own ways. After this is over, whatever happens, go back to the Black Robes."

Adelle watched Reynard. All her hatred had vanished. It seemed so ridiculous, him standing stirring soup as if he were a woman, and yet such a simple thing encouraged her. "Ah, but you would miss me, no?" she said softly in French.

Reynard glanced up, a faint smile stretching the corners of his mouth. "Hmph!" he grunted.

"Perhaps your words to me are wise," Adelle went on. "But you are wrong when you say that you have nothing to offer me. You have offered me your friendship, your protection and your honesty. These you have given from your heart. A heart that is tender, Reynard. There is more to you than Mighty Fox, the warrior son of Old Coyote. You are Marie's son, and the son of the Frenchman she loved. That must mean something. That is what I wanted to tell you." She lay back down and closed her eyes. Her heart was satisfied, and the soft fur robe felt comfortingly homey as she settled her weary body into its nest.

Reynard said no more. But Adelle knew her words had touched him even if he would never admit it.

Three days later, Adelle was strong enough to cook the morning meal and do her chores. She rested when she felt tired, enjoying the spring sunshine after the gloominess of the longhouse.

Mighty Fox cut bark from the elm trees nearby to replace some of the strips on the longhouse. Winter snows and ice had taken its toll on the little dwelling, and the bark was easiest to remove while the sap was running. He spread the bark sheets out to dry and was weighting them down with rocks when Red Earth returned from his morning hunt.

"My friend, did your hunt go well?" Reynard asked, stopping to greet him.

Red Earth smiled. He wore a breech cloth and leggings. A wide ring of fur circled his head. It just fit over his brow, leaving his crown uncovered. "I feared my Wendat brothers had whispered to the animals to hide from their Odawa guest, but finally they honored me by showing themselves to be hunted. I pleaded, 'Do not disgrace me in the eyes of my friends, little brothers,' and they were pleased to come to my aid." He held up two rabbits for them to see.

Reynard laughed. "Those were two that did not listen to their Wendat family," he teased.

Red Earth grinned good-naturedly. "I offer them to Mighty Fox, my friend. Something else also." He reached into his pack and drew out a newly prepared fishing net. "For you, who have been my father while I have stayed among you."

Mighty Fox handed the rabbits to Adelle and took the fishing net. He placed his hand on Red Earth's shoulder. "Stay and eat with us. Share our fire, for it is I who am thankful. Little Turtle would not be standing with us if you had not heard her cry out. Your gifts please me, Red Earth."

Adelle quickly skinned and gutted the rabbits, cooking the meat while the men waited. Red Earth's voice was pleasant, and again she was drawn to it. She found herself stopping her chores often to listen, to watch Red Earth's gestures and how his cheek curved when he smiled.

"It is time for me to return to my village," Red Earth was saying. "I have pelts to trade for corn. Then I will be leaving."

"I wish you well."

"I wish us all well, my friend."

Adelle jerked her head up sharply. Red Earth stared into the distance while Reynard lit his pipe. Adelle had not missed the emphasis in his words and wondered what he meant by it.

Later, Jean Baptiste gathered his pelts into a pile and walked to the post near the village. Tension was building here. The English fueling it with rum. He was glad he was leaving and hoped this wouldn't take long. After an amount was agreed upon, the Englishman poured his corn into a basket. The post was almost empty at this time of day, except for three drunken Wendats and another Englishman sitting alone at a table.

"Right nice pelts you have there," the trader commented as he rummaged through Jean's pelts. "Was a good winter, I say. We'll be seeing more like this soon. Not as thick as the pelts a little ways south though, eh Pierre?"

The other man at the table grunted a reply, and Jean looked again at the lone man. He had brown hair, and his features seemed too delicate to be an English trader, though in manner of dress he appeared to be nothing else. Jean took his pouch of corn and leisurely passed the man at the table. The man leaned back on his stool and in so doing, bumped the table, knocking an unlit candlestick to the floor.

Jean stooped to retrieve it, and as the man reached out his hand to take the misshapen article from him, the sun shown on a silver ring he was wearing on his third finger. The initials P.A. were inscribed in script, tiny, but distinct.

The man nodded his gratitude and replaced the candlestick, leaning back as before and muffling a rum induced belch.

Jean glanced briefly at the man's face then continued on his way. This man was definitely not a trader. Pierre. Jean raised his eyebrows. A Frenchman was allowed in Orontony's village. P.A. Pierre Antoine? Again he puzzled over the familiarity of the name. Suddenly a realization swept over him like a cold shock. Antoine was among the men reported missing in Pontchartrain the day he met with DeLongueuil. He had not been lost in an Indian ambush as his commander believed. He had deserted. A most fortunate convert who knew all things French. Jean clenched his teeth, and he felt the muscles tense in his cheek. He must hurry to meet DeLongueuil's trader.

Reynard walked quietly through the trees until he was far from the village. He wanted to be alone to seek wisdom, just one more time. He needed to be sure of his decision to sit out the war before he left for home. He folded himself down between two large rocks. He sat a long while, replaying the words of Orontondi and Old Coyote, the memory of Yellow Sun. A season had passed he feared, and all things that followed would not be the same. He feared this passing, and wished for courage.

He reached into his shirt, pulling out the letters he had kept hidden in the box under the sleeping platform. They mattered little to him now. He tore them into tiny pieces and buried them where he sat. No matter how hard he tried, he could not rid his spirit of his yandiyonra, his intellect, as Old Coyote advised him. A warrior with a divided spirit was no warrior at all. He could not fight this war. His disgrace shamed him. There was nothing he could do now but leave. He would take Adelle back to Pontchartrain if she wished; at least there was honor to be had in keeping his word.

Reynard suddenly became alert as a small mixed flock of nuthatches, and chickadees, grew quiet and darted away. Cautiously he peered over the rocks, searching the trees. Voices drifted faintly through the young green veil of leaves. He listened intently. Finally, he was able to discern a word or two. DeLongueuil, Nicholas. Reynard stiffened; these men were speaking French. He crept silently to within twenty feet of the two men and nearly cried out in disbelief at the sight before him.

Red Earth spoke quickly in French, gesturing urgently to DeLongueuil's envoy beside him.

"I tell you he is here," Red Earth was saying. "Antoine is helping the British and Orontony plan his attack. He must have deserted. We must send word to all the outlying posts to be on their guard."

Both men scanned the trees nervously as they prepared to leave. Anger burned in Reynard's chest. Red Earth was a French spy. Had he not shared his food, his fire with him? He should have never trusted an Odawa brave, he thought. They were fickle friends.

Reynard narrowed his eyes and drew his knife. He had treated Red Earth as a son, but Red Earth had betrayed their friendship. Now he must kill him. He must kill them both. He leaped from his hideaway with a loud cry, hurling his knife mightily at Red Earth, driving it deep into his shoulder above the heart. He missed his target.

The trader's eyes widened in terror as he lifted his musket.

"No!" Red Earth yelled at him and staggered backward. "Go! Go!" He motioned wildly to the French trader, and the man fled through the trees without firing.

Red Earth gripped the knife and pulled it from his flesh seconds before Reynard flung him to the ground. Red Earth desperately held him at a distance with one arm, struggling to gain a foothold to flip him over.

Reynard was surprised at Red Earth's quickness and strength despite his gaping wound. Suddenly the odds were turned, and Reynard found himself on the bottom, but Red Earth never drew his knife.

"You are a traitor!" Reynard spit at him.

"And what are you, Reynard?" Red Earth panted.

Reynard threw him aside.

"Little Turtle is not your Wendat wife. She is French." Red Earth lay on the ground, blood oozing from his shoulder. "I am not the only one with secrets. What might happen if Orontony discovered this?"

Reynard glared at him.

"We both have secrets," Red Earth continued. "Secrets that endanger us. Why should we kill each other?" He stood and held out his hand, but Reynard got up on his own.

"I treated you as a father treats his son," Reynard said, picking up his blood smeared knife. "You have betrayed my beliefs and have no respect for me." He wiped his knife against his thigh, for the desire to kill Red Earth was gone. "You will never sit at my fire again. I will not speak for you."

"I did not betray you, Mighty Fox. The British are not your friends but your nematrezue. Look what they have done to the people beyond yungtarah. I am doing what is best for many lives. This is our way; the good of many," Red Earth argued.

But Reynard turned his back to him and disappeared through the trees. Surely, he had given up the fight, Jean thought, for Mighty Fox could have killed him easily. He trusted Mighty Fox would tell no one of his discovery because of the young woman. But the hurt in his eyes was something Jean had not expected; something he regretted. "I-ye-et-sa-tigh." I am sorry, he said.

Sinking to the ground and leaning against the base of a hickory tree, he took a strip of deerskin from his pouch and tried to tie a compress of leaves across his shoulder. He knew he must stop the bleeding. Presently, drums began to beat in the distance. He gave a feeble sigh and closed his eyes. Sweat trickled down his back. Perhaps Mighty Fox had revealed his actions to Orontony after all. Perhaps DeLongueuil's agent had been spotted.

He was too weak to run and in no condition to fight. He must hide for now. He held the compress in place which was already sticky with blood. Wearily, he stood, the trees swaying before him. Everything was a green twirling pool. He collapsed in a heap on the cold, damp ground.

Brave Arrow had arrived in the village with a company of braves, and Adelle wished Reynard would return. There was excitement among the Wendat. Adelle was curious, but remained cautious as she followed a group of women to the center of the village. The elders had gathered around Orontony, and it was hard to tell exactly what all the commotion was about. Brave Arrow spoke loudly to all the elders. He had found an opportunity for importance, Adelle thought, and he meant to make the most of it.

"Fathers," he addressed them. "There are five traders not a hawk's flight from here. They come to this village."

His next words were drowned by Orontony's cry. Its shrillness made her shiver.

She retreated to her little longhouse and fell to her knees before the sleeping platform. "Please, please, God make them go away," she pleaded for the traders' lives. Later, when the dogs began to bark, Adelle pulled herself up from the floor and on trembling legs, made her way to the opening in the wall. Standing among the women of the village, Adelle watched, horrified at the sight of five Niagara traders cheerfully greeting Orontony and presenting him with gifts. They had no idea of the danger surrounding them.

"Please, God," Adelle breathed.

Upon his arrival in the village, Reynard saw a throng of gathering Wendats as if a meeting had been announced. He threaded his way through them, straining to see the reason behind the confusion. Finally, Reynard broke through a circle of braves. "What is happening?" he asked.

"French have come from the Guyahoga. Without permission and proud," a young brave answered him.

"Without permission? Since when does a trader need permission to stop at a post?" Reynard said, not waiting for an answer. He pushed through the crowd of young men, but Brave Arrow caught him by the arm.

"Mighty Fox, I thought you would have returned to your village by now to ready yourself for battle. Is it not your way to be where the most honor may be gained?" Brave Arrow smiled, menacingly.

Reynard jerked his arm free. "But you do not surprise me Little Arrow. You are always where there is much anger and very little wisdom."

"Do you say these words to Orontondi, you white? I will kill you someday!"

Reynard backed away. He regretted revealing his thoughts to Brave Arrow.

It was over quickly. Reynard stood gravely taking in the sight before him. Five Frenchmen sprawled awkwardly on the yellow sand. Bewilderment shown on their faces. Surely they had no idea what had caused the reversal of Wendat hospitality. Their gifts were strewn on the ground. These men sought no one's land. They wished enough to eat, enough to drink and a forest to challenge them, not unlike any Wendat man their age. These men were not his enemy, he thought. His enemy was far away, plotting and planning how to conquer and profit, using ordinary, unsuspecting men to accomplish their goals.

"Mighty Fox!" Brave Arrow called to him so all the young braves could hear. "Are you weak in the knees like a woman at the sight of French blood? Is there part of you where your blood still runs thin like these dogs?"

Reynard stood silent before his accuser. He felt the eyes of the Wendat braves upon him as they hushed their cries of victory. He saw Orontondi gravely observing Brave Arrow's challenge.

"Prove your spirit is Wendat, that your blood is thick!" Brave Arrow continued his ranting. "Take a scalp, Mighty Fox. Take a scalp, if you are not weak!" His taunt resounded in the sudden stillness.

Reynard drew his knife from his belt and held it high. He must not falter. To fail Brave Arrow's challenge would mean his death. He stooped over a dying Frenchman whose face was frozen in the terror of death. Blood covered his face and beard.

Suddenly a memory from long ago loomed before him as clearly as if he were a young boy again. He and his father were picking up their trap lines along the Tahquamenon River in early spring. He dropped his father off first, paddling downstream to attend more lines with the understanding that his father would catch up to him shortly.

But in his haste to gather his lines, his father failed to notice the mother bear and her cubs foraging the thicket along the bank. Unfortunately, he had positioned himself between them. On hearing his father's cries, Reynard ran to his aid. By the time he had reached him, however, it was over. The scuffle was brief, but final. Reynard had staggered at the sight of his father. "Help me," his father had wheezed as he lay crumpled on the bank, the blood streaming down his face and beard.

But there was nothing Reynard could do.

Now, Reynard's hand trembled as he clutched his knife. He grasped the man's hair and sliced a thin sweep across the man's skull and around his ears. He peeled it off beginning at the nape. He held up the bloody skin, the Frenchman's black hair still attached and dripping blood.

A loud cry went up all around him. Running Dog joined his scream of triumph with the others, and Reynard was not surprised to see Running Dog's hands were smeared with blood also. The drums beat louder. The women sang. Reynard clenched his teeth together so tightly he thought his jaw would break. The scalps were later carried to the British, and he slipped away as soon as he saw a chance.

He made his way through the darkness, to the river and waded in. The water was cold, but he thought little of this as it rose to his hips, for not even the water could wash away his shame.

It happened so suddenly, Adelle marveled. The Frenchmen had been seized at the urging of the British, beaten viciously and taunted by the Wendat women. The drums beat joyously in the village now. Bravely she walked to the center of the village where the celebrating had reached frenzied proportions.

But she had not prepared herself for the carnal pillaging that was customary among the tribes against their enemies. Bloody scalps hung from a pole, and hideous amputations of the men's bodies were carried about and flaunted. Fearing she was about to faint, Adelle stumbled to the edge of the woods, dropped to her knees and vomited. She remained in the cover of the trees until she had stopped shaking. A vision of Red Earth flashed before her. Surely he could not be among them.

She had not seen Reynard since Brave Arrow's challenge. But it didn't matter anymore. She wanted to be as far away as she could go. Pulling herself up with the aid of an oak sapling, she staggered through the darkness to the river and headed north.

Desperate Flight

It seemed as if a black curtain were draped overhead. No stars shown in the overcast sky to encourage Adelle as she picked her way slowly and silently through the forest, her strength returning. She had no idea how far she might travel or what might happen tomorrow; she knew only that she had to get away from Orontony and his vengeful hate.

The river turned and opened up as it cut its way to the bay. Muffled noises drifted across the water, and Adelle crouched low, wary of the strange shadow that appeared ahead. For moments that seemed hours, Adelle strained to make sense of the whispered voice and the humped shape in the river. Silently she crept closer. She lay flat on top of the bank, the shadow of a man standing almost in mid-stream below her.

"Ho-ma-yen-de-zuit-et-et-rang." God forgive me, the shadowy figure pleaded. "Forgive me. Oh Master of Life, I have walked the only way I know, and I am broken. Show me the path to the healing of my spirit."

The voice floated to her on the soft sweet breath of the night air, and Adelle recognized its familiar tones. "Reynard?" she called softly.

The water splashed in the darkness as the dark shape twisted to face her. "Adelle!"

"What are you doing?" Adelle stumbled down the steep bank.

"I am sorry I brought you here," he said. All the pride and gruffness were gone. "Tonight, I am sorry for many things."

He waded to shore and gripped her by the shoulders. But she backed away, startled by his manner. He had never approached her like this before.

"There is no need to fear me, Adelle. Today, I have no nematrezue."

No enemy. Adelle swallowed hard. "You mean the traders?"

"No. They have killed Mighty Fox the warrior."

Adelle studied him, but it was too dark to see his expression. His words made no sense.

"There are plans to murder the French at Fort Miamis. I must go there and warn them."

"Warn them?" He must be drunk, she thought.

"The river is new everyday, Adelle. New waters, and so there is new blood in me. Go back to the village and bring me my things. I am leaving tonight–"

"You are leaving me here? Alone? Now?" A tingle of fear bubbled in the pit of her stomach.

"Listen to me," he said stepping closer. "Brave Arrow will follow me when he knows I have gone. He will know where I go. He wishes to kill me. You are safer without me, but you must find Red Earth–"

"But he left this morning! He is far away from here!"

"No. I nearly killed him hours ago; he will not be far. Go! Get my packs; you must hurry!"

"What? Why would you hurt Red Earth?" Truly he was drunk, she decided. "Oh Reynard, Brave Arrow will bring a party of braves with him. At least let me go and fight with you."

"No! He will kill me only if he can catch me. Now go!" He gave her a shove toward the village.

Adelle hurriedly retraced her steps and stole into their longhouse. Hiding Reynard's pack and a pouch of dried corn under her cloak, she slipped out of the walled village once again. The drunken revelry continued behind her, but she was sure no one had seen her.

Reynard was already waiting by the water's edge with his canoe. "Be sure to hide your tracks," he told her. "Red Earth will not be far from the two rocks by the old oak. Tell him what has happened and where I have gone."

He took the packs she handed him. "Do not lie to Brave Arrow. Tell him the truth. It will keep you alive. Remember, no one knows you are French. There is no one in Orontondi's village who does. Running Dog is here. You saw him. Do not trust him. Remain Little Turtle to them. "

Adelle's shoulders shook in silent sobs.

Reynard drew her close, resting his chin on the top of her head. "It is good that I go, Adelle," he assured her. "You have been the one wise. But my heart sits at two fires. If I face one, I turn my back to the other. I must do what is right for this season. Do you understand?"

Adelle clung to him now. "Yes. But I cannot do this, Reynard. I am afraid."

"Your God is with you, no?" he said softly in French. "He did not save you from drowning to die at the hands of Brave Arrow. Courage, Adelle. Courage. I was wrong. You have no soft belly under your warrior armor. It is from where your strength comes." Gently he pushed her away. "I must go. Find Red Earth; he will help you."

Adelle wiped her nose with the back of her hand. "After you tried to kill him?" This couldn't be happening. He was leaving her. Fresh tears ran down her face.

Reynard sprang lightly into his canoe. "I thought he had betrayed me. But I was the one who had betrayed myself. He will help you. Now go!"

Adelle waded into the water, reaching for his arm as he lifted his paddle by its throat. "What will you do after you warn the Fort?"

"I will come to Pontchartrain if... If I am able," he finished.

Her hand slid down the side of his arm as he pushed off. Reynard turned the canoe and became only a black shadow against the river as he paddled away, fading into the darkness.

Slowly, Jean Baptiste opened his eyes. Darkness had fallen, and drums beat furiously. Wailing and yipping filled the night air. He rolled over on his side, feeling for his wound. Mud stuck to his shoulder. Fortunately, it had helped push the compress against him. He was still bleeding, but not as much. He tried to sit up, but again he became dizzy; slowly he eased back down.

This will never do, he thought in dismay. Lord, You have to help me! A staghorn sumac thicket was not ten feet away. He rolled into it and covered himself with the low gnarled branches. At least he was hidden from plain sight. It was all he could do for himself at the moment.

How long he lay there he did not know, for he drifted in and out of consciousness. The feasting in the village had nothing to do with him, he decided. Unless of course they had captured DeLongueuil's trader and were torturing him. After a while, he propped himself against the sumac's trunk. The wound was deep but clean, he decided. A little lower and it would have sliced his heart. He had much to be thankful for.

Adelle stood a long time by the water's edge. She bit her lip. "Oh God," she prayed. "Oh God." For no other words would come.

She looked about her. Picking up a handful of dried grass cast aside by the spring flooding, she dusted the ground all the way back to the edge of the woods, then made her way to the big oak. She stood in the darkness listening for any sound other than the drums behind her. Surely, she thought, if Red Earth were near, he would never hear her.

"Red Earth," she called softly. "It is Little Turtle. Mighty Fox has sent me."

Adelle neared the oak and called again, but there was no answer. Nervously, she drew her cloak around her. Perhaps he was able to travel farther than Reynard figured. Maybe Reynard was delirious with rum. Suddenly a branch moved behind her.

"Red Earth?" she whispered, squinting into the shadows.

A man rolled from underneath a thicket and struggled to stand. He did not make it, however, and fell at her feet.

She knelt down and pushed him over. It was Red Earth. Mud was caked to his hair. She touched the dark stain on his shirt, and her fingers came away sticky with blood. He was alive, but he had fainted. Quickly she tore off her cloak and placed it on the ground. Stepping over him, she rolled him onto the cloak and pulled him through the forest as far as she could. Somehow, she must get him back into the village with her. She especially would have to go back if she were not to appear suspicious.

In a small clearing she groped for the plant she knew was there: red root. She grasped it, and pulled it out. She tore off the leaves, stuffing them under the deerskin strip over Red Earth's wound. He groaned as she touched him.

"Msko Aki!" she rasped into his ear, shaking him. "You must wake up!"

Jean gripped her arm. "What is wrong?" His breathing was uneven, but he was coming around.

"It is Mighty Fox," she told him. "He has left to warn Fort Miamis of an attack–"

"Warn them?" He tried to sit up.

Adelle pushed him back down. "Listen! Brave Arrow will pursue him. He wishes to kill him. He will kill me also–"

"Does he know you are French?" Jean demanded.

Adelle fell back, startled at the blunt unveiling of her secret. "No, I –"

"You must go back to the village– Wait." He caught himself. "Why is there feasting?"

"Five French traders came into the village expecting the Wendat friendship as before, but they were all killed..." Her voice died away. If Red Earth knew she was French, did anyone else?

Red Earth was silent for some time. She was beginning to suspect his strength was failing again.

"Go to the creek and bring back water," he said at last. He reached for a leather pouch at his side.

Adelle unfastened it and ran to the small brook nearby, filling the pouch to the top. Red Earth had undone the compress and removed the leaves by the time she had returned.

"Pour." He motioned to her.

She held the pouch over the open wound, pouring the cool water into the wound as a wash. Red Earth cried out in pain, but she covered his mouth with her free hand to quiet him. Gathering more red root leaves for a compress, she replaced the strip of deerskin. Again she filled the pouch with water and raised his head to drink. "Why would Mighty Fox do this?" she wondered aloud as Red Earth gathered his wits.

"We must both go back," he said hoarsely after his brief rest. He raised himself using his good side and stood, holding a branch for support. "Mighty Fox will be missed only after the rum wears off. We have a little time." He sighed, shakily. "Drape the robe over me." He pointed to her cloak on the ground.

She placed it across his shoulders, and he adjusted it so that his wound was hidden.

"Go," he told her. "Go and do whatever you would do if you thought Mighty Fox was celebrating with the other braves. When it is light, search for him. Go to Brave Arrow and tell him Mighty Fox is gone."

"But–"

"You must go to him first. This is important. No Wendat will honor you if you hide Mighty Fox's offense. For it will be an offense. One they will fiercely avenge. Meet me here as soon as Brave Arrow and his war party have left."

"What will you do?"

"I am going to make it look as if I have had a night of the rum. Hopefully no one will remember who attended the feast, least of all a drunken Odawa."

"Do you have strength for this, Red Earth?" she asked as he stumbled weakly ahead of her.

"Hah! The Christ, the God of my life, will give me strength!"

Adelle abruptly came to a halt. Red Earth trusted in God. A surge of hope swelled in her heart. But she said nothing. There was no time anyway as the eastern horizon grew lighter, and she ran ahead of him into the village.

Carefully she made her way around the longhouses and into her own. No one had seen her since she avoided the fires around which sat the more hardy drunken braves. No dogs barked for they knew her. Adelle sat on the bark floor near her smoldering fire. She listened for the dogs or any sign Red Earth entered the village, but there was none. She sat for hours until she heard the village stirring to life. Even then, she was careful to go about her chores as if Reynard were among the braves. Early in the afternoon, and only then, did she venture into the village circle to make her search for Mighty Fox.

"Is Mighty Fox among your men?" she inquired at longhouse after longhouse, and each time the answer was no, they had not seen him.

Running Dog was there with the war party. A band of red moose hair circled his head as an adornment for war.

"Is Mighty Fox among the braves of your village, Running Dog? I have not seen him, and I look for him."

Running Dog shook his head. "Perhaps he has gone to lay his nets."

Adelle nodded and turned to the post. Propped up along the wall was Red Earth, his clothes in disarray and stained with mud and rum. As she passed, the stench of rum was strong, and his sleeves were stained with blood. No one would guess that it was his own, Adelle thought.

She returned to the longhouse and waited a while longer. The sun was warm in the gloomy gray sky when she approached the braves again. Angrily she stomped into their circle around the fire. Running Dog stood as she tossed Reynard's fishing net into his lap.

"He is not fishing as you had thought!" Adelle cried. "Mighty Fox is gone. I have searched for his canoe, and it is not here. I waited as you advised me, but when he had still not returned, I searched his things. His packs are gone!" Adelle scowled menacingly.

Brave Arrow stood scrutinizing her for a long time. Running Dog picked up the net.

"Our brother is near." Running Dog defended his friend. "He is only drunk with rum."

"He is not drunk!" Adelle insisted. "He is gone."

"Hah!" Brave Arrow spit on the ground.

"He is drunk and with a young woman somewhere. I know him."

Adelle grabbed the net from Running Dog, savagely stomping it into the ground. "Mighty Fox is not your brother!" She shouted. "He is gone. Hear me! He is gone."

Running Dog gave her a piercing glare. "Why would he leave? Where has he gone?" Running Dog demanded of the other braves. "He has proven he is our brother. Did he not take a scalp as the rest of us?"

"You fool!" Brave Arrow said. "He knew we would kill him if he did not. He has deceived us, and now he carries his white tongue to warn the fort." He strode angrily to Adelle's longhouse, the braves following him, and he searched the small dwelling for himself.

"It is as she says. He is gone," he told them. "We must tell Orontondi."

Adelle waited beside her cooking platform as the braves entered Orontony's longhouse. She was only a little amazed when Orontony himself made his way toward her.

"Tell him what you have told us, Little Turtle." Brave Arrow pulled her by her arm until she faced the feared Wendat chief.

Adelle formed a hasty prayer, hoping her nervousness would be hidden in her mock anger. Orontony stood mutely as she recounted her story. His eyes narrowed and grew hard with hate. He turned on his heel, and Adelle heard his terrible words.

"Kill him," he said.

Braves whooped and yipped as they ran to their canoes. Running Dog walked behind the others, throwing an annoyed glance over his shoulder at her. He wasn't only angry with her, she knew. He was perplexed by her betrayal

Faithful Running Dog. Surely Reynard had no better friend among the braves. He had defended him, had trusted him, had hoped for the best in the worst of circumstances in spite of overwhelming proof to the contrary. And now as he looked at her, his former bright countenance was clouded by hurt and confusion. As he turned away from her, Adelle believed whatever crime the Wendats would accuse Reynard of, certainly Running Dog had already forgiven him. Adelle was sorry Running Dog would remember her this way, a disloyal, mocking wife. Indeed, he deserved a better leader than Brave Arrow.

Pierre Antoine peered darkly from the doorway of the post. Another racket had begun among the braves. "Now what's happened?" he asked the Englishman.

"One of the braves is missing, I guess," came the answer. "His squaw reported him missing anyways. That's her over there, the young one. Right nice lookin' that one is. They only get a bit soured when they're older, eh?" He snickered a nasty little laugh.

Pierre Antoine gazed across the clearing. He hadn't noticed this squaw before. She was easy on the eyes. He cocked his head to one side. There was something about her...

After the braves had left in their canoes, Adelle endured the sympathetic stares of other women as she retreated to her longhouse. She packed her things into a shoulder pouch and wound her way around the houses, intent on heading for the river.

"Little Turtle!" called an ancient woman sitting next to a cooking platform. "Where are you going?" she inquired suspiciously.

Adelle respectfully stopped in front of the wrinkled hag, her stomach tensing into a hard knot. "To my own village," came Adelle's rehearsed reply. "My husband Mighty Fox has betrayed the People, and I am ashamed to be his."

The ut-sindag-sa smiled, her empty gums gleaming. "You are young, Little Turtle. There is still time for husbands." She laughed. "You are welcome here. The spirits will deal with Mighty Fox justly."

He was already dead to her, thought Adelle.

"I am grateful, Aneheh, but today I long for the comfort of my village. For many days I have waited, and my eyes grow weak from looking for the day I will return."

The woman nodded with a sly grin. "May your journey be successful," she said, holding up her hand in farewell.

Adelle went on her way, biting her lip. This woman thought she meant Yellow Sun's village, and probably figured she had a replacement for Reynard already in mind. She walked the rest of the way with her head down, not wishing to attract any more attention. She neared the post where the Englishmen were standing outside bartering with two middle aged Wendat women. Their conversation grew louder as the women seemed to be refusing to leave the post.

"I cannot give you any more rum," the older Englishman was saying. "You owe me enough already. Now get back to your work or I'll throw you out of here."

"Surely, half a bottle will not break you," the younger man said to the first. "Here take mine then," he addressed the women. "But don't expect another."

The women giggled gleefully.

Adelle jerked her head up sharply. She knew this man's voice.

"You'll spoil them, you will, and then we'll never have us a profit!" the older man grumbled.

Adelle looked them over as she passed.

"Since when have I not protected our profit?" The younger man laughed. He nodded to her.

Adelle gasped. It was Pierre Antoine! She turned away quickly. As soon as she was out of sight of the village, Adelle ran as fast as she could to the old oak. Red Earth was waiting for her.

"Hurry," she said breathlessly. "We must go!"

"Does any one know you're gone?" Red Earth shouldered his pack onto his good arm.

"Just an old woman," Adelle took a deep breath. "She thinks I am returning to Yellow Sun's village." She pointed northeast. "Let's go!" she said and started out on a run.

He grabbed her arm. "There is something you are not telling me." His kind eyes had narrowed.

Adelle jerked free and ran her hand through her greased hair. "It is Pierre. At least I think it is Pierre. But, why is he here?" she asked herself aloud.

"Did he see you?" Red Earth demanded.

Adelle glanced at him. "Yes. But I don't think he recognized me."

"Go!" He pushed her on, furtively scanning the trees, then ran ahead.

Adelle ran too, spurred on by fear, and she had no trouble keeping up with the wounded Red Earth.

Jean Baptiste frowned. He had no choice but to travel overland. He hated to waste the time, but the Wendats were too numerous along the rivers, and Brave Arrow would be searching every route to Fort Miamis. Besides, Jean thought ruefully, he doubted he could paddle for long with his stiff, wounded shoulder. He had many questions for his companion, but they would have to wait. He had to focus on not getting lost in unfamiliar territory.

It was twilight when they reached the large river flowing into the lake. He stood back from the bank in the cover of the trees watching for any activity along the river. All was quiet.

Adelle stood next to him. "How will we cross? We have no canoe," she whispered.

He pointed to the west. "It may narrow farther upriver. We will cross there."

Adelle followed behind him in the darkness. Thankfully a half moon illuminated the night. Soon they were able to forge and swim across, and Red Earth stopped farther inland when they had travelled as far as he could go.

Beads of perspiration shone on his forehead, and he was breathing heavily. "We will rest and then go on. We must travel as far as we are able these first hours," he told her.

As far as you can travel, Adelle silently corrected. She had no desire to stop. She sat on the ground and pulled open her pouch. She gave a handful of pemmican to him and took some for herself. She sucked it slowly, trying to remember what Reynard had said about Red Earth. But she didn't have much opportunity for reflection because he measured her in the same inquisitive fashion that she did him.

But he seemed to be regarding her as a matter of business, not trivial curiosity. He held out his hand for more pemmican. "Who is Mighty Fox that he should suddenly want to warn Fort Miamis?"

Adelle avoided his gaze. She was unsure of how much she should tell him. How did he guess she was French? Certainly Reynard had not revealed her secret. "Mighty Fox is my husband–"

"No," he interrupted, shaking his head. His voice became hard. "I want the truth. He is not your husband; you are not Wendat. Now, I ask again– who is Mighty Fox?" His tone was severe, and in that moment he didn't seem to be someone to be trifling with. He was as fierce as any of the Wendat warriors. Kind Red Earth had vanished.

Adelle swallowed and set down the pouch. Apparently he knew more than he had ever let on anyway. It was of no use to continue the lies. "He is Reynard DuPree," she answered calmly. "His father was French, his mother Wendat, and he was raised with the Wendat after his father's death. Reynard was sent to carry the message of war to the Wendat near Pontchartrain. He came to council as a brave from Yellow Sun's village." Adelle shrugged. "What has inspired him to warn the fort, I do not know, but I think it was the Frenchmen's deaths." Her voice fell as waves of worry tingled up from her gut. She hoped she had given him enough time to stay ahead of Brave Arrow.

Red Earth drank water from his leather pouch then offered the container to her. "Why do you travel with him?"

"I came– I came to read letters for him."

Red Earth was quiet. He hadn't expected this, she thought. She fought back the overwhelming dread of his disapproval. She tipped the soft smooth leather pouch to her lips, letting the cool water flow down her dry throat.

"Letters the traders were carrying," he said accusingly. "News to the forts."

Adelle handed him the empty pouch. "It is not what you are thinking," she said wiping her mouth with the back of her hand. His angry eyes tore at her heart.

"And what is that? That you intercepted information that would warn traders. Traders like those behind us in the village lying in piled heaps on the sand. You betrayed your country–"

"No!"

"Then perhaps Reynard DuPree forced you. Were you captured?"

Adelle did not answer. She would not betray Reynard. "Who are you, Red Earth? Why do you care so much about what I have done? You came to the council– for what?"

Red Earth gave a soft, scornful laugh. "You are loyal to him, I see. Well mademoiselle," he addressed her in French. "Let me introduce myself." He held out his hand. "I am Jean Baptiste, a mètis also. At the moment, I am in the employ of Commandant DeLongueuil, and now we are headed for Pontchartrain."

Adelle gasped. Her mind raced backward. Reynard must have discovered Red Earth as a spy. Betrayed, he had said. That is why he wanted to kill him.

Now to save herself from being charged, she would need to expose Reynard's guilt. This she would not do. She did not shake Baptiste's hand.

"Very well," he said withdrawing his offer. "We will have to get along anyway, yes? It is Pierre Antoine in the village, by the way."

Adelle was stunned. "But why?" she asked when she found her voice.

He fairly sneered. He seemed to be enjoying his role as the herald of her misfortunes. "He is using his um, talents, shall I say, to help the British. It is curious, these acquaintances of yours."

"Monsieur Baptiste," she declared indignantly. "I have not seen Pierre Antoine in almost a year. His presence here has been a shock to me, I assure you. And I am convinced he is not the man I thought him to be." Adelle rose, brushing off her deerskin dress. "I am ready to go. I am as eager to reach Pontchartrain as you are."

Jean stood. "Good," he said gruffly and led the way deeper into the forest.

Late into the night Pierre Antoine sat alone emptying his bottle of rum. It was coarse drink, he thought. No where near his beloved brandy. But as he drained the contents of his glass, he could not erase the young squaw from his mind. The view was hazy, however. He was entering the blissful numbed state induced by his drink.

Peculiar behavior, indeed, he thought with effort. She seemed afraid of him. And yet, he had seen her before somewhere else; he knew it. She turned away from him almost as if she were hiding something. Her image haunted him. It wasn't her beauty. No, he could pick from any of the young women in the village to satisfy his desire for beauty. It was more the inconsistency. It was the charming form, the feminine tilt of her chin and the surprising confidence of her stride, not as a young woman, but more like a young brave. It was like the absurdity of a delicate rose growing from a hardened oak. Like... Like a beautiful young girl growing up in a world of ill-mannered men.

Pierre sat up straight and dropped the bottle on the table. Adelle Chaboillier! And she had recognized him.

Pierre stumbled out of the post, this bit of information quickly sobering him. He staggered to the small longhouse built for visitors, but no fire was lit, and it was dark. He felt the sleeping platform. The furs were gone. He reached into the baskets. The corn was gone. He cursed in French, tearing the baskets from their shelf.

Marching into the Englishman's house, he wrenched the man from his bunk. The man's Indian woman pulled the fur robe over her again, rolling over onto her side, in an effort to ignore the rude interruption of her sleep.

"What's going on here!" the man demanded, trying to open his eyes.

Pierre knelt next to him, his face close to the Englishman's. "That young squaw is working with her husband to foil us! She is gone."

"No," the Englishman said yawning. "An old woman talked to her. She is going back to her village. You're drunk. Go on." The man pointed to the door. "Go on," he repeated.

"That is a lie." Pierre said, giving the man a violent shake and stood up. In the morning, he would speak to Orontony and ask for a few braves to accompany him. He had no choice, but to kill her before she could get word to DeLongueuil of his presence here.

When he had reached the waters of the Maumee, Reynard could not maintain the pace he had set. He had not slept and had eaten nothing. Paddling against the current had slowed him considerably, more than he was comfortable with anyway. A party of braves could cover much more distance than one man. He decided he would have to rest if he meant to go on at any rate at all. He pulled to shore and hid the canoe. He sat down nearby in a spot where he had a good view of the river, but was able to remain concealed by the gnarled undergrowth.

Carefully he lit a small fire and pulled tobacco from a black deerskin bag hanging on his belt. He laid the tobacco on the burning twigs, fanning the smoke on his skin. He sang softly, barely a whisper, but the song died in his throat. Angrily he brushed the tobacco away.

Visions of bloody Frenchmen haunted him. Of his father. Of Old Coyote. Of Adelle, shaking and vulnerable on the shore of the bay. He held up his hands, looking at them as if for the first time, hands that were dirty with shame. They had murdered, sometimes for the Wendat, sometimes for himself. But this had been in battles, tribe to tribe.

The five traders were innocent of any offense Orontondi imagined, and even though Reynard had no part in their death, the guilt of the crime overwhelmed him. Had he not hastened Orontondi's plan? The French had misused them, yes, but... he wasn't ready to murder men like his own father. He realized this now. Too late, he thought bitterly.

He had not thought of his father in years. Now he knew he had deliberately tried to forget. Losing him had hurt like nothing he had ever known since. Old Coyote had helped, helped Reynard to forget that he was French. Reynard knew Old Coyote did what he had thought best. But deep in his heart, Reynard could never really forget.

A new season had begun. He stretched out face down on the cool sand. He would never be cleansed of these men's innocent blood. Never.

"God," he spoke the name the Jesuits preached. "I do not know You. Surely, I do not know how to speak. Do not be angry with me. But if You are the one God, God over all gods as they say, teach me. Show me the way I am to go, for I have never walked this path before. Bring the words spoken to me to my ears that I may remember. Forgive me. I have no offerings to give You. Only myself. I offer my spirit to Yours that I may be filled with Your wisdom."

The water flowed melodiously in the distance, bringing life to the forest, and so the Spirit of the Living God came to him, bringing new life to his thirsty heart.

In the early morning light, Brave Arrow studied the bank along the river. A fine mist hung over the water, but it did not hide the night's secret. He motioned for the braves in the other canoe to pull in with him. The thicket here had been disturbed. Farther in, he found tobacco leaves half burnt and strewn on the ground. Mighty Fox was not far. He returned to the canoe.

"He is near," he told the braves in the two canoes. "I can feel his presence."

They paddled with new strength. All but Running Dog who sat helplessly in the stern of the second vessel, dragging his paddle through the water as if a great rock were tied to the end. The sun was high when a canoe was spotted up ahead. The closer they came, the harder Brave Arrow drove in his paddle. It was Mighty Fox.

Reynard saw them over his shoulder and tried to out distance them, but it was no use. Brave Arrow drew his bow.

"I am honored this day!" he cried, positioning his arrow.

But his aim was high, and the arrow flew over Reynard's head. Reynard stood up carefully, brandishing his war club as they drew alongside. The braves were upon him. Suddenly, he was struck in the back of the head by Brave Arrow's club. Reynard fell back into the water, and two arrows pierced his side below his heart. Face downward he floated, and the swift current carried him away and pulled him under.

"A-a-a-e-e!" Brave Arrow cried fiercely, deftly climbing into Running Dog's canoe. He tried to turn the craft around as if to go after Reynard's body, but Running Dog held him back. He peered over his shoulder now, but there was nothing to see. There was no sign of Mighty Fox as if the river swallowed his body and he had never been.

"Mighty Fox is dead," Running Dog told Brave Arrow as they both watched the river behind them. "Our enemy lies unsuspecting before us." Running Dog pointed upriver. "Let us go and take more French scalps to honor the Wendat."

Brave Arrow pushed Running Dog away and grabbed Reynard's paddle. He sat at the bow with Running Dog behind him. As if enlivened by their revenge, the party of braves propelled their canoes upstream, fairly gliding over the top of the water on their way to Fort Miamis. Running Dog looked back once more, but the river revealed nothing of its secrets. He glanced at the braves around him, his comrades, his brothers. Their faces were aglow with the joy of triumph.

Far downstream, Reynard's body caught in a tangle of brush at the side of the river. The current washed over him and gently flipped him over.

Pierre Antoine watched the old Indian guide carefully. He hoped he was as skilled at following a trail as the Wendat had promised.

"This way," the old man said. "She keeps to the cover of the trees." He pointed out a small limb on a sapling that had been bent as something brushed past it. He knelt down examining the damp earth.

"Here," he directed.

Pierre knelt beside him. A small track, barely visible to the common eye, took shape as the old man outlined it with his finger.

"The front of the moccasin only," the Indian said. "They travel fast."

"They?" Pierre inquired.

"A man travels with her," he answered standing and pointing up. About three feet ahead and a little over six feet off the ground, tiny branches smaller than his little finger drooped from the limb of an oak. They were bent back and so that the yellow wood under the bark showed.

"How far ahead," Pierre asked, impressed with the man's observations.

"Less than two days, perhaps."

Pierre rose to his feet, a faint smile spreading across his thin lips.

❦ Despairing Hearts

Adelle followed Jean north to the Toussiant. The air hung heavily in the early summer woods, and black bugs swarmed annoyingly in the air over their heads. Others bit at any exposed flesh. Now and then he held aside a branch for her as they passed through a tangle of vines, for he avoided the trails as much as possible. But he said little, and his manner was sullen. Adelle walked quietly, her eyes fixed on the young man in front of her. She longed for his understanding, but the facts were unforgivable in his eyes.

The setting sun cast the forest into a dappled array of gold and green shadows. As soon as it was dark, Jean lit the wood Adelle had gathered, and they fanned the smoke over themselves to ward off the insects. It was swampy here, and there was no higher ground to retreat to. They had no dried puccoon to mix with bear grease to cover their skin either.

She reached into the bag she carried at her waist and pulled out the bulbous roots she had dug earlier. She brushed them off and laid them next to the small fire. She sat close enough to the heat to keep most of the biting hoards at bay. She stole a glance at Red Earth through the snapping flames on the other side of the fire. He was packing more leaves under the cloth over his wound, and his hand came away wet with fresh blood. His face seemed drawn and his eyes heavy. It must have been difficult for him to continue their arduous pace. Adelle hoped he could get her past this southern region of the Erie. From there she would be able to make her own way.

He wiped the blood on his leggings, and looked up at her. "Don't allow yourself to hope, mademoiselle," he said with an evil grin. "I won't die before we reach Pontchartrain."

Adelle watched the yellow flames dance between the logs. She had seen enough of death, but there was one question she needed to ask. "Why do the People..." Her stomached tightened. "Why do they..." She closed her eyes briefly, trying to shut out the butcherous visions, but they were seared onto the inside of her eyelids it seemed. Words failed her.

Jean turned the bulbs over in the fire with a stick. "You mean why do the People carve up their victims and eat them?"

Adelle turned to him.

"Sometimes, they eat them."

His tone did not hold the horror she thought it should.

"Because they believe a man's power is contained in his flesh and blood," he said. "When they defeat their enemy, they gain this power by torturing or eating him. It makes them all the more powerful." He shrugged. "A priest once told me there is power in the blood. What you saw back in the village was The People's version of that idea."

Adelle turned away from him. She wanted to ask which version he adhered to, but she pulled her thoughts to bear on the cheery warmth of Papa's little cabin. How she wished for its comfort. Instead, she sat on strangely cold soil indeed.

"You said my name in Odawa."

She watched the small flames.

"Back there. Outside the village. You called me Msko-aki. You speak Odawa?" He poked at the roots with his stick. Prodding them. He expected an answer.

She lifted a shoulder and let it drop.

He raised his chin. "Hmph."

"You are used to travelling," Jean commented reaching for his share of the food when it had roasted.

Adelle bit into the root. "I travelled with my father. He was a trader. Some days we went very far."

"And where is he now?" Jean asked sarcastically.

Adelle stared into the fire. "He is dead," she answered quietly.

Jean watched the firelight flicker in the leaves above them. "I am sorry," he said.

She nodded and said nothing more. Surely, he did not mean it, she decided, since he thought her to be a traitor. This kindness to her was only politeness, and she sincerely wished she would have remained Little Turtle in his eyes, eyes that had looked upon her and smiled. She spread her blanket on the ground and lay down. She could not bear the expression he held now and wished sleep would hide her shame.

Jean fanned the smoke over him again, envying the light's glow as it touched Adelle's tawny skin. Her hazel eyes were closed in sleep, and he could gaze openly now on the beauty that had stirred his spirit since he found her at the edge of the frozen river.

But his envy was mingled with anger and sorrow. She loved Mighty Fox, he thought bitterly. At first he had been relieved to discover they were not husband and wife, and yet, the matters of the heart were not settled with ceremony, he realized. They were determined by choice. It was clear her loyalty to DuPree ran deep. What else could bring this effect but love? He wanted to believe in her innocence, but the truth was she was a traitor to her own countrymen, innocent women and children. This he could not ignore.

His heart sank when he remembered the softness of her touch, the sound of her voice when she spoke his name. But these things were not his to remember. They belonged to another man, a man who did not deserve to have her. He tossed the root into the fire and stretched out on the ground. He would rest, and before it was light they would move on.

Adelle opened her eyes to the darkness. The fire was almost out, she observed groggily, so she must have been asleep for some time. Then she saw dirt had been scattered on the embers. Eerie silence met her ears. She looked for Jean's familiar shadow, but could see nothing. Suddenly the rustle of branches exploded into the night air, and Jean leaped with a cry from the darkness behind her as strange shapes erupted from the undergrowth. He held the two figures at bay for mere seconds until one tore from the fray and headed for her.

"Kill him!" Jean ordered her in Outawae.

Adelle jumped up, grabbing a fallen limb that she had placed near the fire and swung it with all her might at the dark shape rushing towards her. She hit squarely, and her attacker stopped in his tracks. A Wendat war cry sounded behind her as Jean continued his struggle. Her attacker reached for her. Driven by fear, she swung again, fiercely. He slumped to the ground, and Adelle saw he wore a British trader's coat. A pistol fell from his outstretched hand. Hastily Adelle scooped it up, ready to try firing should Jean be unsuccessful.

Jean wrestled the other man back and forth in the darkness. Finally he gained a foothold, throwing the man from him and back into the brush. He attempted to pounce upon him, but the unknown attacker escaped into the woods, disappearing into the inky darkness.

Jean roughly grabbed the pistol from Adelle and pushed the man lying on the ground over with his foot so that his face shown in the dying light of the fire. Adelle gasped and fell back, her knees buckling beneath her. It was Pierre Antoine.

"Is- is he dead?" Adelle could scarcely speak.

Jean breathed heavily from exertion. Blood was seeping from his shoulder again. He looked at her. "He came seeking a young woman, but he met a warrior. His fate was not by your hand. It was by the judgment evil requires."

His words were hard, spoken as one used to dealing justice to men. But she pushed herself backward across the scuffled ground, away from Pierre. Jean rifled the Frenchman's pockets, emptying the contents into his pouch. He fumbled with the pistol.

"It jammed. Come." He motioned with the pistol. "We must go quickly. They know our plans."

Adelle stood on shaky legs and followed behind him ever wary of another attack.

Days passed, and soon they travelled familiar territory. They were in the Outawae hunting grounds, and the pace quickened considerably. Jean traded his coat and the pistol for a canoe. Soon they were headed into the open water of the Okswego.

Adelle was almost sorry, for she had nothing to look forward to. She knew Jean was a man of duty. He must bring her before DeLongueuil. But even at this, she respected him. It had been a difficult journey from the start, one she would remember always for the gentle Red Earth who had saved her life not once, but twice. Since he now considered her a traitor, she wondered if he regretted his kindness. It was a question that pierced her heart.

Finally they reached Pontchartrain. It set on a rise, above the Teuchsagrondie River or DeTroit as the French hailed it, and it almost looked as if it were ready to fall into the water it was built so close to it. The fort was surrounded by log walls of upright poles carved to a point at the top and standing well above her head. One gate opened to the river, and there was a gate opposite it on the west wall and one on the south. They were double hung gates made from logs in the same fashion as the walls. Pontchartrain was similar to the Wendat villages, but it had strong lookout towers constructed at all four corners, and inside were row houses built in the same upright log fashion as the wall.

Jean reported to DeLongueuil as soon as they arrived. The commandant's house stood just inside the west gate and was larger and finer than Adelle remembered. She bit her lip as they entered. The massive slope-topped twin fireplaces both opened to either side of the room, and the walls were slathered with white plaster. The door behind them was paired with another on the opposite wall, creating the middle point of the house and the distance between the hearths. She stood next to Jean, nervously twisting the fringe on her belt and waited for him to relate her part in this treacherous affair to the commandant sitting at his table.

"Monsieur Baptiste," DeLongueuil addressed him as he stood. "I am pleased all has gone well with you. It was reported you had been killed. I am very happy to see otherwise." He shook Jean's hand. "I've received all your information, but I am greatly alarmed that one of our own countrymen has aided in the attempt of our demise. We were warned a while ago by an Indian woman about the attack planned on Pontchartrain. Is this still their intention?"

"Yes, Commandant. Orontony has called his council for this purpose. He has united the nations in the area as one against the French. You know them as Miamis, Huron, Pouteaouatami, Shawnee, Saulters, Nadowessioux and Outawaes. There are some bands within these people, however, that will not join with him."

"May God have mercy on us," the commandant said, glancing at Adelle. "And your Chief Macinac is loyal to the French?"

"Yes, Sir. He has changed his mind concerning any friendship with Chief Nicholas."

The commandant nodded approvingly. "He has declared this, yes, but–you understand," he finished apologetically.

"Yes. Also, Orontony has slain Frenchmen from Guyahauga," Jean continued. "Five traders stopping on their way north were captured and killed."

"Who murdered these men?" the commandant's voice turned hard.

"A war party at Sandoskè."

"I will demand those murderers be brought here! I need to send some one right away. Cursed it is, yes? Traders have been worried ever since Chaboillier's murder last fall."

Adelle stiffened.

"Good man," the commandant went on. "He was friendly to the tribes; can't imagine what happened. LeClere found him covered with stones behind his post, a hole in his chest from an Indian knife. A trapper passing through must have buried him. He had a daughter, but we never found her. Captured by the Miamis probably. Poor child is probably dead by now."

Jean was quiet. He studied the plank floor and fingered the small quills of his knife sheath. Adelle could only guess his thoughts. But he was not an imbecile, and it was probably quite clear to him she was the murdered trader's daughter. She forced a calm passivity.

"Is there anything more, Monsieur Baptiste?" The commandant laughed bitterly. "As if five murders, a treacherous deserter and a war are not enough!" He cursed.

"Yes," Jean answered slowly.

Adelle bowed her head. This was the moment she had dreaded, for she knew in her heart she could say nothing against Reynard, the man God had chosen for Himself. It would mean her execution.

Jean lifted his head. "The Frenchman, Antoine, he is dead."

"Hardly a tragedy, no?" the commandant replied. "I will thank you for it. It saves me the trouble."

"I am not the one who struck him down. She did." Jean nodded to Adelle.

"Brought down by a woman. There is justice, my friend! What is her name?"

Jean gave her a withering glance and turned to the commandant. "She was introduced to me as Little Turtle," he said.

"Thank you, Little Turtle." The commandant bowed. "All of New France thanks you."

Adelle was shocked by Jean's unexpected act of mercy. She wished he could know her gratitude, but his icy demeanor stilled her confidence.

"A gift? Should I present her a gift, Jean?" DeLongueuil asked.

Adelle quickly tipped her chin to her chest. It shamed her to even consider such a thing.

"No," Jean said gruffly. "I have brought her to Pontchartrain as she asked. That is all the trade she wished." He turned to leave. He seemed tired of the whole affair suddenly.

"Thank you, Monsieur Baptiste." The commandant offered his hand, and they shook once firmly.

Jean passed through the doorway, and after a quick glance at the commandant, Adelle followed him. Surely, Jean could have given her over to the commandant as a traitor, and she would have been promptly executed.

"Jean," Adelle said catching up to him. "Thank you. I–"

"Why didn't you tell me the truth?" Jean whirled around to face her, his eyes narrowed in contempt.

"I was afraid for Reynard. He–"

"Hmph," Jean scoffed. "Yes, Reynard. Did he murder your father?" Jean raised his eyebrows sarcastically. "He must have a habit of leaving knife holes in people. I have finished what I have been asked to do. I must go."

Adelle's heart sank at his rebuke. She grabbed his arm as he turned away. "No. He did not kill Papa. Reynard thinks it was the Miamis, eager to begin the war and gain supplies for themselves. He kept me safe. I feel no guilt in what I have done for Reynard," she said softly, trying to hide the hurt his words had brought to her. "Not anymore. I was led on the path which lies behind me now. It has changed me, yes, but I too have finished what I have been asked to do. The hand of God has been upon me, Jean. My heart is clean before Him."

"What will you do here?" he asked. His voice was strained, and he avoided her gaze.

"I will go to the Jesuits and wait for Reynard. He said he would come. Do you think he is safe?"

"Hmph," Jean smiled faintly. "I know no other warrior with stronger medicine than Mighty Fox. He lives," Jean assured her. "The feeling in my heart says it is so."

Adelle eyed him curiously. His flat tone puzzled her. "What will you do?" she asked.

He kicked the loose sand in the road with the toe of his moccasin. "I will go back to my father's farm. I am his youngest son, but after his death, he wished that I would inherit it, to keep his name on this soil. I will honor his wish."

"Is the rest of your family there?"

He kicked at the dirt again. "I must go," he said, turning away without looking at her.

She watched him walk toward the tall gates of the west wall, and a throng of children of various ages, fort resident and habitant, ran toward him, a skinny five-year-old girl with flowing black hair easily leading the pack. Jean scooped her up and sat her on his shoulders as he was engulfed by the rest of the children, and then Adelle lost sight of them in the crowd of soldiers just arrived from Montreal.

A wave of sadness rolled over her. Already she missed his presence. Slowly she wandered past the corner of Rue de St. Louis to the church. It was easy to find. A cross adorned its roof near the door and could be seen even at a distance from outside the fort.

Pontchartrain was a busy place compared to other forts. It was the most important one in the area besides Missilimakinak to the north. Both forts were created to regulate the fur trade, but the Jesuits used them as their centers for mission work to the Indians. The church door was open, and Adelle stepped in. She frowned as her eyes adjusted to the gloominess of the room. It was small, with no windows and sturdy wooden benches, as many as could fit comfortably, were lined up in neat rows. A man knelt in the front near a crude altar. He had dark hair, what was left of it, as it was so scarce on top that his skin shone through.

He turned his head slightly, finished his prayer and made the sign of the cross. "Bonjour," the Jesuit greeted her and rose to his feet. His beard was full, dark and well trimmed. He wore a long black robe with the narrow band of his white shirt collar showing at the neck all the way around. He came closer, his robe flowing about him as he walked.

He was medium height and skinny she decided with one look at his hands. His long thin fingers were like the forks of a twig as he carried his hat. He seemed ashen in color. Surely his health must be poor, she thought. His robe was cinched at the waist, and its long flowing sleeves only added to the picture of gauntness. He slapped his wide-brimmed black hat on his balding head.

"Bonjour," she said quietly. She was already pitying this man. She did not know how to go about asking for a place to stay and food to eat.

He smiled kindly. "Are you from the Huron village?" he pointed in the general direction of Old Coyote's village.

"No," she replied, shaking her head. "Saundustee."

"Oh." The priest drew his brows together in bewilderment.

"I came with Jean Baptiste."

"Jean Baptiste? I know him." The Jesuit smiled warmly. "If he sent you here, you must need a place to stay, yes? Are you hungry?" He motioned for her to sit down, and he retrieved his pack from the bench up front. He pulled out a hunk of bread and offered it to her.

Adelle took the bread, breaking off a piece for herself. "Merci," she said.

"You speak French so well," the Jesuit complimented her. "You have spent much time among the French, yes?"

She debated if she should tell him the truth of her identity and decided against it. Adelle bit off a chunk of bread and nodded.

"Perhaps you could be of help to me." The Jesuit stroked his beard with his bony fingers. "You see I had just arrived here from Montreal when I became ill. Gravely ill. It has been weeks since I have visited outside the fort. Today I only travelled to the habitants, and I am worn out. I have not been able to learn much of the savages' languages." He paused.

Adelle sensed he was weighing his next words carefully.

"Would you travel with me?" he asked at last. "I need someone to interpret. My own work has been briefly among the Ojibwa farther north. I do not speak Iroquois. I would also need some one to cook and plant–"

"I will help," Adelle cut in. "But I will only go to the villages near the fort. No farther. Two days at most." She had no intention of allowing herself to be considered a slave as so many Indian women were to the French, or the black-skinned women and children she had seen in other forts with Papa.

"Oh." The Jesuit's dark brows shot up. "Of course. There is a small storage house." He pointed. "You can sleep there. I do not use it much."

Adelle got up and walked out into the bright sunshine. The storage house set back a little ways from the church. She turned to the Jesuit who had followed her outside. "It is good," she said.

"Wait!" he called as she set out for the tiny cabin. "What is your name?"

Adelle turned around again, brushing a stray hair from her face. "I am Little Turtle."

"It is nice to meet you Little Turtle. My name is Father Francois. I have made stew." He jerked his thumb over his shoulder. "You are welcome to eat."

"Merci" Adelle said and resumed her inspection of the cabin.

But there wasn't much to inspect, Adelle thought after pushing open the door and stepping inside. Snowshoes hung on the wall, blankets were piled on a shelf, and a lone paddle leaned against the wall in the corner. It would do nicely though, she decided. She propped the heavy wooden door open with the paddle to let in fresh air and walked to the Jesuit's quarters built onto the other side of the church and accessible by a small hallway.

His cabin was plastered on the interior walls and had a separate room for his bed. A fireplace was built into one wall for cooking and heat. Adelle crossed the room and peered into the pot hung over the fire. A meager stew only half filled it. She bent low over the bubbling brown ooze, grimacing at the smell. She dumped three handfuls of dried corn from her waist pouch into the mess and stirred. It seemed a pity to waste the corn, she thought. Tomorrow she would get them real food.

It wasn't long before the Jesuit regained his health, and Adelle was thankful that he asked no questions concerning her arrival at the fort. Father Francois was in personality a kind, good humored man, and she was grateful for his hospitality and glad she could help him. Fortunately no traders ever gave her a second look, even though some were friends of her father and regular visitors to his post. Because she travelled with the Jesuit, she was considered off limits. She was grateful for that.

Other Jesuits visited the fort on occasion, and Father Francois let it be known she was a most beneficial aide to him. She taught him what she could of Huron and some Pouteaouatami besides cooking, sewing and planting a garden in the narrow plot behind the church that would please even the most skeptic Wendat aneheh. She travelled with him on his treks to the nearby villages and was accepted as his slave. That was fine with her– as long as the Jesuits had no such delusion.

Jean Baptiste came to the post once or twice. He wore his hair loose now, and he had abandoned the Outawae dress for leggings as any other trader. The only giveaway to his heritage was his bare chest, for the Outawae preferred very little clothing in summer.

Adelle saw him and he saw her, but he kept his distance. She grieved at what he must think of her, and her days were long when she let her mind wander, imagining the tenderness of his touch as his hand brushed hers, and how his eyes were full of the sun when he smiled.

Daily she watched for Reynard, but her hope waned as days turned to months. Word had come in that eight traders were captured near Fort Miamis, and one trader had been killed along the Maumee. Other reports, unconfirmed as yet, said there were more traders killed, captured, and property destroyed at various locations. DeLongueuil had sent his military to reinforce the forts because at Missilimakinak trouble had come also. He warned the habitants, French farmers living outside the fort along the river, to take refuge at Pontchartrain. Some came, but the neighboring tribes declared they knew nothing of an attack and denied any connection with Orontony.

Adelle mulled over these things as she went about her daily chores. On a hot, humid day when the sky was a milky white and a haze hung pulsating in the sun's heat, Marie came to Pontchartrain.

Adelle ran to greet her. "Marie!" she called.

Marie turned slowly and squinted in the blinding heat. She raised her brows in mild surprise as Adelle waved to her.

"Salut," Adelle greeted her.

Marie smiled kindly. "It is good that you have returned to your people." She pointed to Adelle's skirt. "I will bring your clothes. I have kept them for your return."

"Oh," Adelle said looking down at herself. " No one knows who I am here."

Marie frowned.

"They believe I am Wendat."

"Has Reynard told you to do this?" Marie said still frowning.

"No. I have not seen him since he left Orontony's village two months ago."

Marie studied her. "Come," she said finally. "I am too old to bake in the sun like bread." She took Adelle's hand and led her to sit in the shade of the church.

"Now tell me what has happened," Marie instructed, and Adelle related everything, including Jean Baptiste and Pierre Antoine.

Marie reached over to untie the eelskin that held Adelle's hair in place. "You are Adelle Chaboillier. You must not hide from her any longer. Your spirit is weak because it is lost and has no where to live. When I come again, I will bring your things. No longer will you wear the dress of a Wendat. It is needed no more."

Adelle grabbed her arm. "Has Reynard come to the village? Have you heard if he is well?"

Marie stared hard at her, and Adelle became frightened.

Leaning forward, Marie touched Adelle's cheek with a calloused hand. "Daughter, Reynard is dead." Her heavy lidded eyes sparkled with tears.

"No." Adelle shook her head. "I do not believe it." She sat up straight, but the force of Marie's words quickly drained her strength.

"Brave Arrow has killed my son. My people say Reynard is a traitor, a weak mètis, but I am proud of him, Adelle. He has found his place, and his spirit rests. I believe this."

"No. He is not dead. I will not believe it," Adelle said, shaking her head again and taking back the eelskin. She stood up. "I will watch for him," she said pointing to the gates.

Marie struggled to rise. "Even when Reynard lived, Adelle, he always came and went as he wished. In this, he was his father, Adrian DuPree. Many days I would grow weary watching for him. When Reynard was young, the times were good. But when Reynard was old enough to become a man, my eyes became sore, my heart heavy, for they both left. Finally, Chaboillier brings my husband's death back to me, and forever my heart waits to be with him. Then my only son was taken from me by my brother, and I did not recognize him as my own. He was changed. Today, my men rest, and I am alone."

"I will wait," Adelle declared with some force. She no longer wished to be in Marie's company as the strain of keeping her composure mounted.

Marie said nothing in return, but it was obvious she pitied her. As soon as Marie had taken her leave, Adelle escaped into the privacy of her little house, shut her door and sank to the floor. Tears streamed down her cheeks. She smothered her sobs by covering her mouth with her hand. It is not true, she told herself. It is not true.

Time passed painfully. Her hopes struggled in a thick sea of despair. She performed her duties oblivious to the world around her, and food held no interest. She cried to God from the depths of her soul, but no assurance came. She longed for the sound of Red Earth's voice, for his touch. She knew the Jesuit watched, silently wondering, always praying.

Three weeks later Adelle carried a basket of newly harvested corn into Pontchartrain to be dried for the Jesuits. The harvest had begun and the habitants generously supplied their priests. As she reached the church entrance, a commotion could be heard coming from the commandant's house. A crowd had gathered, and Adelle wandered closer, curious to the cause of such a ruckus.

"What has happened?" she asked another woman standing near her.

"A trader has brought in a murderer!" the woman replied.

"A murderer?" Adelle repeated, trying to see around the taller men in front of her.

"Yes," the woman said. "They say he murdered the old trader, Chaboillier!"

Adelle nearly dropped her basket. She pushed her way into the half circle forming a hedge of onlookers outside the commandant's stoop. Her heart beat wildly. She took a deep breath to calm herself and broke through the last wall of people.

A man lay on the ground, a Frenchman. Adelle had not expected this. Mud was plastered to his cropped black hair and beard. Grime covered his body and leggings. A hideous scar rose in a mound of mangled flesh on his stomach which was seeping with blood from fresh tears in the old wound. His hands were bound, and traders took their turns kicking him in the sides and head and spitting in his face. His ribs shown through his flesh, and Adelle could barely stand the torture of this pitiful man, Papa's murderer or not.

A shadow fell over his gaunt form.

"He is one savage who will never murder again." A familiar voice addressed the crowd of traders.

Adelle jerked her head up so sharply it hurt. Jean Michel LeClere stood on the commandant's steps.

Adelle looked again to the man on the ground. It was Reynard DuPree.

Paths of the Righteous

Adelle covered her mouth with her hand. Two soldiers grabbed Reynard, one on either side, and dragged him up the steps and into the commandant's house.

Adelle was jostled by the men gathered around her as they strained to hear the voices inside the house. But she ignored their jeers and vengeful enthusiasm. Reynard needed help. She knew of only one person who could accomplish it in this crowd– Jean Baptiste. They would listen to him.

She must find him and bring him back with her, she thought. She dropped her basket on the grass and ran to the habitants' farms outside the fort along the river.

The habitants' farms spread far in either direction along the shore, and Jean's was the last on the north fork, nearest the Outawae village. She ran the whole way, dodging mudholes along the steep bank, until she came to a small house, its narrow plot winding far inland and rich with a late summer harvest. Adelle squinted into the afternoon sun. A wisp of gray smoke rose from the chimney, and two musquash hung near the open door.

"Monsieur Baptiste?" she called, timidly. She saw no one. "Jean?" she called again. She peered into the cabin, but it was empty. Walking around to the back she called again. This time she could see a man in the fields, and she ran out to where he stood picking corn. "Jean!" she called as she came near him.

He dropped the ears of corn he held into a basket on the ground. He seemed surprised at her visit.

"I-I need your help," she stuttered, breathlessly. "It is Reynard. He's been charged with murder."

Jean pressed his lips together firmly and looked into the woods at the side of the field.

"He is innocent, Jean. I know," she said softly.

He made no reply, and Adelle waited fearfully as he picked another ear and stared into the trees again. His silence surprised her. She had not considered he might refuse her plea.

"He is charged with Papa's murder," she said. "The men, they will listen to you."

Jean looked down at her. His eyes were dark, and they held an expression Adelle could not describe. She had never seen it before.

"Please," she barely whispered. "Help him." She squirmed beneath his stare.

Finally he broke his awful silence. "I heard he was dead." He didn't seem sorry.

"No." She shook her head. "He cannot die," she said, her voice tight. She blinked, clearing her eyes of tears.

"Tell me the truth– all of it. No more of your lies." His words were stiff and cold.

Adelle nodded, gladly relating everything from her move to the little post along the Rivière aux Raisias with Chaboillier and her desire to go to see Antoine, to her meeting Reynard and her time among the Wendat. She told of Yellow Sun, Brave Arrow and Reynard's last words to her.

She took a deep breath. "Reynard once would have attacked the French. But he respected my father, and he wished me no harm. I was safer with him than I would have been with any of my father's friends. And my reading letters– it came to nothing in the end because the man who forced me to do it was the same man who risked his life to warn Ft. Miamis."

"But what if the forts would have received the letters, Adelle? The envoys didn't know the contents." Jean was quiet as he fingered the broad leaves on the cornstalk beside him. He sighed deeply. "You are the only person who can speak for Reynard," he said. "You," he told her, raising his head. "Adelle Chaboillier. Not Little Turtle."

"But–"

Jean shrugged. "There is nothing I can do." He picked up his basket and walked to the house.

Adelle followed him. "Will you come with me, then?" she begged as he set down the corn. She looked up into his eyes and was confused at what she saw. Perhaps he did not believe her. And why should he, she thought. She was suddenly sorry she was weak, sorry she felt she needed him.

She raised her chin higher in an attempt to restore some of her dignity. "I know–" she said and had to bite her lip to keep it from trembling. "I know when we met you found me in a lie. I was not Wendat. I was not Little Turtle, wife of Mighty Fox, and you discovered I interpreted for the Wendat against my own countrymen."

She laughed weakly. "You have no reason to believe me. You saved my life and have brought me to Pontchartrain. That is enough." She turned to go. "I should not have come. Forgive me," she said and walked back down the road toward the fort.

Jean Baptiste ran his fingers through his long hair. His heart was heavy in his chest, and his emotions churned his stomach. He was not bound to Reynard. Mighty Fox had advanced the war which resulted in the death of the traders, even if he did not kill Chaboillier. He was guilty. Of many things, Jean thought bitterly. Yes, the unrest stirred by the British was general knowledge even to far flung posts. Traders were always at risk in the lakes region whether they acknowledged it or not. The letters would have added caution, however.

The memory of the pain in Reynard's eyes after he discovered "Red Earth's" betrayal nagged him. He had come to respect the man he knew as Mighty Fox. He liked him. A Wendat. Who may have changed his mind about supporting the uprising, but too late to matter. Hadn't he warned his brothers about their fickle nature?

And Adelle. She was telling the truth. Perhaps that was why it hurt. Forgive me, she had said. He already had. Of everything she had done or ever would do. He loved her, and no matter how he tried to quench his passion, it would not die. But she had come to love the Wendat mètis. Jean hit the side of the house in frustration.

Whatever his feelings were toward Adelle, they were in vain. But he could not deny her happiness, even if it was joined with Reynard DuPree. He could not respect himself if he did not try to help them. He grabbed his shirt off the peg by the door and walked the path to the fort as the sun dipped behind the trees.

Adelle broke into a run as soon as she was out of Jean's sight. DeLongueuil may decide Reynard's fate quickly, and she knew what she must do. She slowed to a walk as she neared the commandant's house. Marie's words echoed in her ear. You are Adelle Chaboillier. Daughter of a trader. You must not hide from her. Hadn't she told Reynard the same thing practically? Before she had judged Reynard; at this moment, she understood how easy it was to avoid painful memories by hiding from the truth.

She realized with growing clarity she had remained Little Turtle not only for Reynard's sake, but because she was afraid to face her future as Adelle Chaboillier alone. Adelle gazed into the fading light of the evening sky. Already the white moon hung gracefully overhead.

"Only in Your mercy," she whispered to the Heavens as she approached the soldier standing by the commandant's stoop.

"Monsieur," she said to him. "I need to see the commandant. I know this man the trader brought in."

The man studied her a moment, then disappeared into the house. When he came to the door, he motioned for her to enter.

DeLongueuil rose from his carved chair and pointed to a stool near his table. "My officer says you have something to say about this man." He jerked his thumb in Reynard's direction. "You are the woman Baptiste brought with him, yes?"

Adelle looked past him and saw Reynard was slumped on the floor against the wall. His chin touched his chest, and his shoulders drooped wearily. His face was swelling from his recent beating and fresh blood trickled from his forehead and the side of his mouth.

Adelle sat down. The room was quiet, and she could hear the blood pulse through her ears. "I am...," she began, but faltered as the commandant regarded her queerly. She swallowed. "I am Adelle Chaboillier." Her voice was barely audible.

The commandant raised his eyebrows.

"This man," Adelle continued with a glance at Reynard, "did not kill my father."

The commandant tapped the expensive tabletop with his fingers, looking first to Reynard and then to her. "Yes?" he said tilting his head back. "You know who has murdered your father then? And you like a ghost among us. Why have you deceived us all this time?"

Adelle eyed him curiously. His tone was mocking as if he did not trust her. She was only a "squaw" to him. One from Reynard's own territory, after all. He had good reason to suspect her.

LeClere came from the corner of the room. He leaned close to her, the breath from his nostrils reeking with brandy. He scowled disapprovingly.

"Monsier LeClere," the commandant demanded. "How long did you know Chaboillier and his daughter?"

LeClere pulled himself up in a show of importance. His filthy clothes marred the effect, however. "Almost ten years."

"Is this Adelle Chaboillier?"

He leaned toward her again. "Hah!" LeClere shot out, his breath hot and disgusting in her face. "Some little Huron squaw," he sniffed.

"Monsieur LeClere," Adelle cut in. "The last time I saw you was October previous; my father met with you in the attic loft while I shelved some of the supplies. You brought a letter to my father from Ducharme. You informed us you were leaving for the Kankakee, and my father ordered 300 plank nails."

LeClere grabbed her hair and pulled her head back into the fading light. He examined her even more intensely than before, and Adelle cringed at the closeness of him. Suddenly he released her.

"F-Forgive me, Mademoiselle Chaboillier," he stuttered, stepping back into the shadows. "I did not recognize you like this!"

DeLongueuil stared at them both. He tapped the table again and crossed his arms over his chest. "Mademoiselle Chaboillier," he said at last and bowed slightly. "Who killed your father?"

Adelle returned his stare. "I do not know. I was downriver at the Pouteaouatami village, and when I returned– he was dead."

The commandant rubbed his chin. He chuckled. "Forgive me. If you do not know who killed your father, how do you know it was not this man?" He pointed to Reynard.

Adelle hesitated. "Because he told me that he did not," she said at last.

"And you believed him, yes?" He nodded with an air of dignified arrogance.

"Yes," she answered, tipping her head back defiantly.

"Hah!" The commandant laughed. He pushed his chair aside. "Well, let me tell you what I know of Reynard DuPree!" he shouted as he paced in front of Reynard. "That he lives as a Wendat brave. A brave who wished to annihilate the French in the forts and the traders in all of New France. Men like your father! Women like you!"

"That is not true!" Adelle cried. "Reynard wished to warn Fort Miamis."

"Eight French traders were seized at Fort Miamis," the commandant said, leaning over the table toward her. "One Frenchman was killed near there. I think he did not wish to warn them, mademoiselle, but to carry their scalps to the British!"

Tears threatened to flood her eyes. She clenched her teeth. Reynard continued to gaze at the floor in resolute silence, and she wondered what horrible thing had stolen his spirit.

DeLongueuil continued his arrogant glare. "You were brought here by Jean Baptiste from Orontony's village. How did you get there?" he demanded.

Adelle faced the commandant. To answer him would only seem to prove Reynard's guilt.

The commandant pressed his lips together in a wry smile and crossed the room. His actions were no longer smooth and polished but jerky. "Your silence tells me more than you wish. I am not a fool." He turned around. Anger had brought a flush to his face. "Were you captured?"

Adelle did not blink.

"Were you captured by Reynard DuPree?" he asked sternly.

"No–"

"You were captured by Reynard DuPree after he murdered your father!" the commandant interrupted.

Warm tears dropped onto her cheek as she shook her head. "Please, Monsieur Commandant–"

The commandant's voice softened as he came near her. "Do not be afraid, little one. Just tell the truth, and he will never harm you again." His expression was full with fatherly compassion and acute mercy.

"No, please," she insisted shaking her head. "You must understand. I-I went with him willingly."

"No!" Reynard suddenly shouted. He struggled to get up.

"She is lying!" LeClere's voice boomed across the room, and he shoved Reynard to the floor.

A sound at the door distracted the commandant. Adelle turned to see Jean clearing a path through to the threshold.

"It is all right," the commandant assured his officers outside the door who were not able to hold Jean back.

"Commandant," he addressed DeLongueuil and bowed his head respectfully. "Excuse me sir, but I heard your conversation." He pointed to the open doorway. "If it pleases you, I will speak."

"Yes." DeLongueuil motioned for him to continue.

Jean paused as he looked long and hard at the changed Reynard now lying on his side, his face turned to the wall. "This woman is speaking the truth," he said to the commandant. "I too heard that Mighty Fox, as his Wendat family have named him, left Orontony's village to warn Miamis. A war party went in search of him, and it was reported they had killed him in revenge." He strode past LeClere and knelt next to Reynard.

"Truly, the scars on his body were not made by a gun or knife, but by an arrow." He fingered the wound. "Perhaps two. What trader or soldier kills his enemy in this way? I believe she speaks the truth."

DeLongueuil bent down to inspect Reynard's scar. Jean pulled Reynard to a sitting position and grasped his shoulder.

"Commandant, this man discovered I was a spy, but he did not reveal his knowledge to the Wendat." Jean stood. "I was able to return unharmed and report to you because of his silence. He advised this woman to travel with me because he was anxious for her safety. I did not know she was Mademoiselle Chaboillier. I can only attest to the Wendat's concern for this woman, and his trust in me to bring her to the safety of the fort.

"Men," he addressed DeLongueuil and LeClere, "is it difficult to understand that if a man came upon a young girl alone, he might take pity upon her with the knowledge of Orontony's war sounding in his ears? Would we not do the same?" He waited for his words to settle in their consciences. "Wasn't the old trader friendly with DuPree?" Jean asked LeClere.

DeLongueuil turned to LeClere. "He was," DeLongueuil answered.

"Truly, she was dressed as a Wendat not to deceive us, but to deceive the Wendat."

DeLongueuil was thoughtful as he walked to the one window in the room. "She said she went with him after her father was murdered."

"Were you friendly with DuPree?" Jean looked at LeClere.

The commandant scoffed. "None of us are friendly with him."

"That may be the point sir," Jean said. "Is it wise to accept the testimony of a man's enemy, or the testimony of the murdered man's daughter?"

The commandant turned from the window. Adelle could see him thinking, and Jean certainly had his attention.

"Surely, you cannot believe that a man who loved his daughter as much as Chaboillier must have, would be betrayed by the object of his love?"

Adelle marveled how quickly Jean's calm manner had brought order back into the room. She wiped her tears and wondered what had made him come. He stood taller than these men in the room, she thought. Not only in size, but in wisdom. She owed him much. Now, so did Reynard.

Reynard sat leaning against the wall, his head turned to watch Jean, but his expression was a mask to his thoughts.

DeLongueuil sighed. "Is this what happened, mademoiselle?" He walked back to the middle of the room and sat in his chair. "You met him after your father's death; then after finding out Chaboillier was murdered, he kept you with him for your safety until he could no longer provide it for you." He ran his thumb over his brow and sucked air into his nostrils. "He sheltered you in a Wendat village and then sent you to the fort for your safety?"

The last words were uttered in a rush. They seemed to pain him. "Yes," Adelle replied.

"I would like nothing better than to rid myself of this quarrelsome pest!" the commandant declared. "There is nothing to charge him with, however. I have no witnesses against him."

Adelle pressed her folded hands together harder and forced herself to stillness. She wanted no one to see her rising hope.

"I am a witness–"

"To what Monsieur LeClere?" the commandant interrupted him. "You were miles from Chaboillier's post when he was attacked. You are witness to suspicion nothing more. There are so many raids in the area, we cannot blame one man. One half dead at that. I am letting him go. But," he turned to Reynard. "This is your one pass at mercy. If you come before me again at odds with the fort, without a shadow of hesitation I will hang you. Officer!" he called. "Release Monsieur DuPree."

"I pray he dies before he can taste his mercy," LeClere muttered.

Jean stepped aside, and Reynard stumbled as two soldiers led him from the house with Adelle following behind.

"Bring him, please." Adelle motioned for the man to help Reynard to the Jesuit's house beside the church.

Looking over her shoulder, she saw Jean standing outside the commandant's house. He was watching them cross the dusty street. He did not appear to be in very good humor in light of the fact his testimony had freed Reynard. He had come after all, Adelle mused, for reasons she could not guess. She raised her hand in an effort to express her appreciation, but he did not return the gesture. Surely he hated her, she despaired. To such a man, she must seem a pitiful, lying coward.

Adelle and her entourage entered the Jesuit's quarters, and after the officers had left, Adelle motioned for Reynard to sit. "I will get you something to eat and clean your wounds," she told him.

Reynard sank to the floor beside the fireplace like a melting lump of butter. Adelle dipped the large wooden spoon into the steaming pot and filled a bowl with venison. She cooled the broth and spooned it into his mouth. A rustling of cloth made her turn around. The Jesuit had returned from the Indian village.

"What is this?" he inquired kindly as he entered the room.

"This is my friend, Father. He has journeyed far, and he is hurt and weak. I thought he might stay with you."

The Jesuit smiled at Reynard. "She feeds your stomach; I will feed your heart."

The priest helped Adelle clean and dress Reynard's wounds, but it was weeks before Reynard regained strength, and even then he was not the mighty warrior who had danced at Yellow Sun's fire. The wounds in his side were deep, and the Jesuit said it was a miracle Reynard was alive. His healing progressed though, under their watchful care.

Early one morning Adelle and Reynard sat near the outside cooking fire. She had just finished changing Reynard's bandages when Father Francois greeted them from his doorway.

"Good morning, Reynard," he said with a nod. "Adelle, I wanted to travel to the other Huron village today. A habitant told me they have sickness there, and I have some medicine that may help. I am not sure of the way, however. The corn is high, and I have only been west once. Could you–"

Adelle smiled. "I will go with you." The Hurons were known for growing tremendous crops of corn, and fields stretched for miles around their villages.

"You know the way?" Reynard asked in Wendat, only half teasing.

"I can find it as well as you," she replied lightly in flawless Wendat. She tossed him his shirt.

"I may stay a few days," Father Francois said to Reynard almost apologetically.

"I can get along as well as any woman," Reynard assured him gruffly, throwing Adelle a taunting glare.

"I am ready," Adelle informed the Jesuit and slipped past Reynard.

"Au revoir," the Jesuit waved over his shoulder.

Reynard raised his hand in farewell.

Adelle and Father Francois travelled west from the fort on foot, and with a silent prayer, Adelle snaked her way through the maze of cornstalks and into Old Coyote's village just after sundown. As they neared the walls, Adelle began to grow anxious at what kind of greeting she would receive from the old chief.

She did not have to wait long to find out, for while the dogs were barking their usual warning, Old Coyote strode regally out to greet them. Adelle took a deep breath as she passed the empty bear cage. Apparently the young bruin had met his fate. She hoped she would fare better.

"Ne-at-a-rugh," Old Coyote greeted them, but Adelle detected a certain chill in his smile.

"He is welcoming you as a friend," she interpreted. She avoided Old Coyote's intimidating stare.

"Bonjour," the Jesuit answered. "I heard there is sickness here. I have brought medicines for your people." He patted the fat pouch slung over his shoulder.

Old Coyote looked to Adelle, and she related the Jesuit's offer. He did not seem impressed.

"The ceremony is about to begin," he said. "You must sit among us and wait for the spirits to do their work. If all is well, your gift will be greatly honored." Old Coyote turned away as Adelle told Father Francois his words. He seemed in a hurry to return to the villagers.

"What ceremony?" the Jesuit asked.

Adelle shrugged and motioned for him to follow Old Coyote. They made their way to the center of the village where a feast was being prepared. If the old chief had reservations about their visit, the villagers did not seem to share his skepticism. A hearty "Ho! Ho! Ho! Ho!" rang over the village, and the Jesuit looked nervously from one Huron to the next.

Adelle smiled. "It is a welcome," she said.

Father Francois raised his eyebrows in relief. He was ushered to a place of honor near the fire. They were left alone for some time, visited only by curious children, as preparations were being made. The Jesuit drew his journal from his cloak, and Adelle glanced once or twice at the sketches he made of the children. She smiled to herself in a superior way. The priests always seemed to carry these small black books in which they endlessly wrote the "savages'" myths and legends, recording their dress and likeness in strange drawings. Some were realistic. Some were just French versions of half-naked people in animal skins with painted faces.

Two men came to sit with the Jesuit, and a boy joined them. He was not much younger than herself, Adelle thought, but he was also a son of Old Coyote and given respect by the other men.

"Icar-tri-zue-egh-har-taken-ome-enu-mah." I do not like white men he told the two older men with a glance at the Jesuit.

Adelle ignored his rudeness and haughty glare. She determined not to cower in his presence and met his glare with one of her own until he looked away.

She scanned the crowd for a glimpse of Marie, but it was not until the drums began that she spotted her near one of the longhouses. "Excuse me," she pardoned herself to the Jesuit and weaved her way through the villagers clustered around the steaming pots and roasting bear meat. "Marie!" she called over the beating drums and festive singing.

If Marie were surprised to see her, she certainly was an expert at hiding her feelings. She waited as Adelle came nearer. "You do not belong here," she said flatly in greeting, her glance sweeping downward over Adelle's clothes.

"I had to come, Marie," Adelle said cheerfully despite the stinging rebuke. "The Jesuit needed a guide to come here, and, I have good news!"

Marie remained dubious, her expression as warm as a buzzard's.

"Reynard is alive."

There was a passing flicker of emotion in Marie's eyes, but she regained her composure. "So it is true?" she demanded. "We heard what I thought was a rumor."

"He is staying with the Jesuit at the fort. I understand why the story about his death went around. He was hurt badly and barely alive when he arrived."

Shadows flickered on the longhouse wall behind Marie as more wood was added to the fire. The dancers were ready to begin.

"You will stay with me," Marie announced.

Adelle smiled. She was hoping Marie would offer. "I will come later. The Jesuit, he is looking for me, see?" She pointed through the crowd.

Father Francois was now positioned a polite distance away from the goings on as the dancers took their places. He was leaning side to side, peering this way and that as if searching for someone. Marie nodded and melted into the throng of onlookers as Adelle returned to the Jesuit.

Grotesque masks covered the dancer's faces, and a chant began as they twisted about as part of the dance. The orange flickering light of the fire flashed ominously across the hideous expressions of the masks. High pitched shrieks and wails pierced the air, making goose bumps climb up Adelle's arms.

"Graces! It is as if we are in Satan's very lair," the Jesuit declared none too steadily in a hushed whisper.

"The masks are to scare away the evil spirits so there will be no more sickness," Adelle explained just as quietly.

He lifted his chin in understanding and scribbled hastily into his black journal. He paused, his writing hand hovering over the page as he studied the dancers. "It is demonic, that is what it is," he informed her and attempted to copy the various forms of the dance into his book.

Adelle threw him a concerned glance. She hoped he would be a bit more compassionate, at least diplomatic, in his conversation with Old Coyote. The old chief was bound to be offended by such frankness, and the influence the Jesuit desired would be lost. Old Coyote was doing what was available to him to help his people.

When the dance concluded and Old Coyote had finished his duties, Father Francois was brought to sit with him.

"Show me your medicine," he demanded, and Adelle relayed his words to the Jesuit.

Father Francois pulled a flask from his pouch and handed it to the chief. Old Coyote held it up, inspecting it closely. He pulled the stopper and sniffed the contents. Instantly he frowned, clasping his eyes shut. Apparently he considered it rank beyond words. Replacing the stopper, he handed the flask back to Father Francois.

"We will wait one day and see whose medicine is stronger," Old Coyote said. With that he motioned for Father Francois to follow him. Later he and Adelle retreated to Marie's longhouse.

But it was not one day. Four days later the stricken Hurons showed no signs of recovery. Some had grown worse. One died. Father Francois's medicine was finally allowed to be administered by a begrudging Old Coyote. In no time it seemed, the patients recovered. On the morning of the sixth day Father Francois joined Adelle and Marie for corn cakes in Marie's longhouse.

"The people say it is by magic that you have done these things," Adelle informed the Jesuit.

"Are you surprised?" Marie asked him as he chewed his corn cake thoughtfully. "They are not slow to understand. But it is not by miracles alone that you will win them, but by your words. Your actions and your words."

"What would they understand?" he asked Marie. "I need someone to help me, to make them see the need for change–"

"I am not their heart," she replied flatly. "I cannot say to their head, 'This is what you must think.' But I know their ways, and these I will tell you. It is up to you to speak what they will understand. It is up to you to act in ways that will gain their respect."

Father Francois grinned sideways at Adelle. "Very well, Marie," he said, but Adelle hoped he would listen to her.

Marie drew a folded pile of clothes from a shelf along the wall and rearranged a deerskin thrown on the floor as a tarp. She straightened and handed the pile to Adelle. "These are for you," she said.

Adelle unfolded the newly made clothes carefully. They were made like her old ones– a daintier version of Papa's jacket and leggings. But these were sewn by an expert hand, Adelle thought as she admired the craftsmanship. A bit of red quillwork decorated the lapels of the jacket. A new skirt was included also. "These are fine," she said in admiration. "These are very fine. Thank you."

Marie smiled faintly. "I made them as a gift for Adelle Chaboillier."

Adelle did not miss the hidden meaning in her words. She smiled. "I do miss her sometimes."

"Perhaps you wish to return to the fort?" Father Francois directed his inquiry to Adelle as more of an offer.

"Yes," she nodded. "I do. I will leave today. Now, I think." She swallowed the last of her corn cake, brushing her crumbs from her skirt. "But how will you return?"

Father Francois rose to his feet slowly. "Someone will escort me, I'm sure," he said with a wink.

Adelle gave Marie a quick hug and shook Father Francois's hand as he offered it.

"Thank you, Adelle," he said. "Good journey; God goes with you."

Armed with a few messages to deliver for the Jesuit, Adelle left. She made good time, arriving a bit before dusk at Pontchartrain. As she crossed the yard, she saw Reynard sitting in front of a fire he had made outside her cabin.

"So you lost the Jesuit," he remarked with his familiar sarcasm when she was close enough to hear him.

"No." Adelle smiled. "He is still in the village. I came back by myself because Marie has agreed to help him." She peered into the cooking pot. Corn soup bubbled nicely, and she stirred it. "I am tired of corn," she announced. "I am hungry for some of Papa's musquash stew."

"Hmph!" Reynard grunted and filled his bowl.

Adelle smothered a smile. It was good to have him around again.

The Jesuit returned not many days after. Two young braves accompanied him to the fort, and Adelle settled back into her daily routine. One day Marie came for a visit. Reynard was showing Father Francois how to construct a Huron fishing net which he considered superior to all others when she arrived.

Adelle tapped Reynard's shoulder when she saw her crossing the street. "Marie comes," she told him.

He and the Jesuit stood as Marie approached, and Reynard waited for her to speak first.

"It is good," Marie said. "I have waited long to see this day."

Adelle understood the happy satisfaction imbedded in her words. She was not just glad to see her son alive, but that he was among the living ones, the ones who heard and accepted the life Christ was willing to give to all.

Reynard made no reply. He was not being disrespectful, Adelle thought as Father Francois looked upon him rather queerly. It was their custom.

Marie inspected Reynard's bandage, examining it with a mother's eye. "Hmph," she grunted approvingly, sounding much like her son. She pulled a small bark box from her waist pouch. "Here," she addressed Father Francois. "Put this on the wound every day."

Adelle peered over the priest's shoulder. The box was filled with a salve made from herbs and bear grease. Marie insisted on preparing the evening meal, and Adelle helped when she was allowed. When they had eaten their fill, Marie settled herself next to the fire where she spent the night. In the morning, however, Adelle found her tying her pouch to her waist and folding her blanket as if she were getting ready to depart for Old Coyote's village.

"You are not leaving?" Adelle declared, taking Marie's blanket so she could adjust her little pouch.

"I must," she said simply, ignoring Adelle's obvious alarm at such a prospect.

"But you just got here," Adelle objected. "Please stay." She gestured toward her own cabin.

Marie shook her head. "I do not belong here. I am not needed. In my village, they wait for my harvest– my help. You understand this."

Adelle looked down at the ground. In her heart she knew Marie was right, but she missed the sense of family she had experienced among the Wendat. She grinned good naturedly and laid the blanket over Marie's arm. She tapped her own chest in the Wendat way. "I will look forward to your visits, yes?"

Marie smiled. Slowly she walked the path across the clearing and out through the fort gates.

A pang of loneliness washed over Adelle as she watched the old woman leave. "Papa, you would like her," she said more to herself. And sadly, she returned to her chores.

The summer was slowly drawing to a close, and late September's golden glow blanketed the fields and the forest around the fort. By now Adelle realized the truth in Reynard's words to her that night on the river near Orontony's village. The part of Reynard that was cold, hard Mighty Fox was indeed dead. Adelle was amazed at the interest he held in the Jesuit's teaching. This was no small miracle in itself, she knew.

As autumn neared, Adelle busied herself with preparing for winter. Reynard fished in the river outside the fort now and then, and he began preparing trap lines for winter. It was still early in the morning as Adelle placed the last of the squash inside out of reach of marauding rodents. She heard Reynard calling her and turned just as he appeared in the doorway holding two large fish. She took them outside and gutted them, throwing the meat into the pot hanging over the fire in the Jesuit's hearth. Reynard followed her.

"The man of God tells me Red Earth used to come often to the church," he said. "But the summer has passed without his coming. I have waited patiently, but no Red Earth."

Adelle glanced up, continuing to stir the pot to a boil. She added a wild onion.

"I wish to see him," Reynard went on. "Do you know the village where he lives? Is it far?"

Adelle wiped her hands on her deerskin jacket and pushed her long hair to one side. "His name is Jean Baptiste," she said, beginning to braid her hair, not greased in the Wendat fashion, but as she had worn it before. "He does not live in the Outawae village. North," she said with a nod as she busied tying her braid. "With the habitants."

Reynard sat down slowly and was quiet for some time. He stared absently into the burning coals and waited for his breakfast.

"Have you seen your friend here– the warrior you wished to marry?" he asked when the meal was ready.

Adelle blew out a breath of air in a scornful laugh. "Yes, I've seen him. And Papa was right," she added handing him a bowl of steaming corn soup and fish. "He was trouble," she said.

Reynard reached for the bowl, watching the steam spiral into the cool morning air. "What do you think of Red Earth?"

"Jean Baptiste," she reminded him.

"Yes, Jean Baptiste," he said with a glance to her. "The Black Robe speaks highly of him." He held the bowl in one hand and tipped it to his lips. His hair was longer now, and it had begun to curl at the back of his neck. He chewed slowly waiting for her to answer.

Adelle stirred the pot and filled a bowl for herself. She took a spoonful and shrugged again. How could she tell him she liked a man who hated her? What would Papa think? First Antoine and now this. She felt her face growing warm.

Reynard set his empty bowl in front of him, drawing his pipe from his belt. "I want you to go to Jean Baptiste. Tell him I wish to see him."

Adelle picked out a fish bone. "You should go. See his farm," she said, tossing the offending item out the door.

"You have been there?" Reynard leaned forward with interest, giving a brief glance in the direction of the fish bone.

"Once," she replied and emptied her bowl.

"You go," he said leaning back again. "I will wait with the Jesuit." He lit his pipe.

Adelle shot him an annoyed look. Apparently he was feeling well enough to give her orders again.

Reluctantly, Adelle plodded along on the road leading to Jean Baptiste's. The sun was high, and goldenrod gleamed in the fields. Sprinkled among them were deep purple ironweeds. The scenery did not cheer Adelle, however, as she approached Jean's house. She was apprehensive that her coming would not be received well– again.

Surely, he had come to the fort only in regard to Reynard, the duty he felt to return the favor Reynard had bestowed upon him by keeping his secret. In doing so, he had just happened to help her. Something he obviously had no desire to do.

Adelle straightened her jacket and rapped on the door, her mind drawn back to the business at hand.

"Out here!" a voice called from behind the cabin. Adelle grimaced. She was hoping no one would be around.

She followed the side of the house and turned the corner. Jean looked up from his work. He was gutting fish and preparing the meat to be smoked. He eyed her new clothes, giving her a swift appraisal head to toe and toe to head.

"Salut," he said going on with his task in an effort to hide his interest in her change of appearance.

"Salut." She watched as he filleted the meat, casually tossing the scraps into the fire. Adelle smiled, remembering Reynard's reaction the last time she did that.

"Good fishing this morning," he said. "I plan on having a feast. And– I saw a turkey ranging closer and closer. Soon he will be on my table as well." He snickered to himself.

Adelle wished she could remain in that moment, watching him work and listening to him talk, and not irritate him with another request.

Jean glanced up at her. "Is Reynard in trouble again?"

Adelle chuckled. "No." She brushed aside a stray hair. "He asks to see you."

"Oh," Jean nodded. "He is still weak then?"

"No," Adelle replied. "He is much better, but he is not a mighty warrior yet." It occurred to her just then that Jean had never offered his doctoring skills to Reynard.

Jean wiped his knife with a cloth and placed the last of the fish in a basket. "Why did he not come himself then?"

"I do not know," Adelle said forgetting to hide her irritation with Reynard. "He gives me orders like I'm his slave."

Jean turned around sharply and raised his dark brows. "Hah!" He laughed heartily. "I will come. I have things to trade anyway."

He disappeared into his house and returned with a large pouch slung over his shoulder. He handed her the basket of fish. "For Father Francois," he said.

"What about your feast?" she asked with wide eyes.

Jean shrugged. "It gives me an excuse to go fishing again." He guided her back to the road.

His arm swung freely when he walked, and the bag slapped gently against his white trader's shirt. It seemed his shoulder had healed well, Adelle observed. His tanned skin appeared darker next to the shirt, and his straight black hair hung loosely over his shoulders. Adelle walked beside him, her head barely reaching his shoulder. It felt good to be next to him again.

"You are happy at Pontchartrain?" he asked as they strolled the dirt path.

"Yes." Adelle nodded. "It is much bigger than St. Joseph– that is where I grew up– but it is good to be among the French in a fort again."

Jean looked down at her. "No more Wendat disguises then?"

She chuckled. "I guess not, unless you hear of another war they are planning."

Jean laughed. "Good," he said smiling. "That should save me a lot of trouble."

Adelle looked up at him and returned his smile.

When they reached the fort, she led him to Reynard who still sat smoking his pipe beside the hearth fire. The Jesuit was no where in sight, she noticed. Reynard motioned for Jean to sit.

"It is good," Reynard began. "My heart has grown lonely for your voice."

"It is good to see you strong." Jean touched his hand to his chest and thrust it outward to illustrate his words.

Adelle was about to leave when Reynard raised his hand.

"Adelle, prepare him something to eat," he told her. Reynard did not wait for a reply, but again turned to Jean.

Adelle sighed and went to get flour to bake more bread. Jean and Reynard talked by the fire all afternoon. Adelle served the bread and went about her chores. When evening came, Reynard encouraged Jean to stay and eat, and when it was dark to share the fire he had lit outside. The Jesuit did not return as was his custom at times, so Adelle scraped the bowls after supper, preparing to retire to her own little house. But Reynard urged her to stay also.

"Come," he told her. "Sit as we used to last winter, and we will warm our hearts. Many things have happened on our journey together. We are full with these memories."

Adelle sank gracefully to the ground opposite Reynard, and Jean sat to her left, stirring the glowing embers with a thin stick.

"I am grateful for my journey," Jean said quietly.

Reynard nodded, and Adelle watched them, the firelight casting long shadows on the ground. She sensed something between these two men, a feeling perhaps, not entirely amicable, and Adelle searched their faces for answers, but she could learn nothing. The mood was distinctly grave though as Reynard smoked his pipe and passed it to Jean.

"I am also grateful," Reynard was saying. "For these are the scars of Mighty Fox." He pointed to the bare wounds at his side. "The Creator has given them to me that I may not forget his kindness. That I may not forget I was born of two worlds."

Adelle and Jean watched as Reynard lifted his hands to the sky. He seemed at that moment not to be talking to them, but to his God. He turned to Adelle. "I am also grateful for the warrior, Little Turtle who would not let me forget. Truly, Te-main-de-zue, the God above all gods, had planned our paths to meet. He knew we would need each other."

Adelle smiled. "A-au," she agreed. What would have happened to her without Reynard? She didn't want to think of it.

"I am grateful for Red Earth who has led me along the path I now walk," Reynard continued. "Without you, Little Turtle would be lost because of my foolishness. Without your courage in the face of my ignorance, I would not have found the strength to stand against Orontony."

Jean stirred the embers, his gaze fixed on the leaping flames.

Reynard studied them both. He seemed to be in deep thought. "Long ago," he said, "when I was a young brave, Old Coyote instructed me to take a wife."

Adelle leaned forward. Never had Reynard disclosed his family life among the Wendat to her. Never did he reveal anything unless she had pried. Now, for him to speak of something of his past was such a divorce from his usual demeanor, that curiosity prevented her from any attempt at polite reservation.

Reynard seemed pleased with the interest he had generated and went on. "The young woman I desired returned my affections," he went on, "but her father, a man of lean character, would have none of it." He chuckled. "His daughter would not marry a mètis, chief's son or not, and so it was arranged for her to marry another. After a while, she agreed. I could not blame her. But I did wish that she had defied her father. I did not like him and neither did Yellow Sun."

He shrugged. "It was best, I suppose. Perhaps a mètis may never be thought of as an honorable chief or elder. One worthy of everyone's respect anyway. And now that I am older, I am pleased to go as the wind blows the sand." He reached for a handful of dirt and let it trickle through his fingers. "Today, though I have no wife, I am pleased to have a daughter."

Adelle smiled, her eyes bright in the firelight. "Papa would be grateful," she said to Reynard. "He had kind words for you."

Jean lay down. He seemed tired of the conversation and covered himself with his blanket. It was blatant rudeness to an elder, and Adelle was surprised

Jean would do such a thing. But Reynard spread out his mat and did the same.

"My one regret in not marrying is not having a son." Reynard's voice trailed up into the sky full of twinkling silver stars. "Perhaps Ta-main-de-zue has plans for this too."

Adelle looked to Jean, but his eyes were closed, his black lashes and long hair shining in the firelight. Clearly, Reynard was holding out his hand in peace, but Adelle contemplated the reasons this would even be necessary. And even more amazing, he was uncharacteristically patient with Jean's insulting behavior. Reynard had invited him here for a purpose, what– she could not imagine. Adelle sat gazing upon the two men long after they were asleep until at last she withdrew to her own house.

The next morning Jean left after presenting them with gifts of cloth and a blanket. But it seemed more out of politeness than true friendship. Adelle took down the venison strips from the drying rack and packed them into a crock for the Jesuit. Reynard approached her as she came from his house.

"I am going to Old Coyote's village today," he informed her. "I do not know when I will be back."

"Oh," Adelle said trying to hide her disappointment.

He handed her his pipe. "It is all I have that was ever worth anything."

She took the pipe and looked up, unable to hide her thoughts. Perhaps he was not coming back.

"I want you to keep it for me."

She nodded, tipping her head to her chest.

"You did not think I could stay here?" Reynard placed his hands on her shoulders. "You have nothing to fear anymore," he said giving her a friendly shake. "I thought you wanted to come to Pontchartrain, remember? Where is your courage? Where is the warrior?"

Adelle could not answer. She remembered when he left her standing alone in the river.

"Would you rather go back to St. Joseph?" He lifted her chin.

"No. And I do not know what has happened to my courage, Reynard. I think I buried it with my father."

"That is not true, Adelle."

She couldn't stop her tears. "All I know is that you are my friend, now my father, and you are leaving. I fear what I did not know to fear before. Is it a coward who admits this? I miss Papa." She shook her head. "Poor Papa. It was selfish of me to wish to come here and leave him. I feel older now, and my courage escapes me. I know I trust in God, yes? But I do not look forward to being alone. It is a weakness in me."

"Hmph. To wish company is not a weakness. Why do the trappers come running to the posts like starved men after a winter of isolation? I understand their need. And you are not alone as you think," he assured her. "Jean is here."

Adelle scoffed. "He hates me!"

Reynard stepped back in surprise. "Hah!" he bellowed. "He hates me she says! Hah!"

Adelle frowned. His eyes widened in amusement at her reaction. Then he carried on, slapping his legs and laughing as if she had just told a hilarious joke. He was making her angry.

"Are you blind, Adelle?" he asked when he had gained some control of himself. "Do you grope in the darkness like the mole?" He chuckled. "I have endured his love-sick eyes over you like an aging father since he carried you back to Orontondi's village. Truly, if you were my wife, I would have thrown him out like the thieving rat in the basket of corn!" He laughed again. "He couldn't hide his interest when he tried."

"What are you saying?" Adelle cried. "Haven't you witnessed the disgust he shows for me? I went to him for help, to give testimony of your innocence, and he refused me."

"Would it please you to help someone you loved, when you believed your actions would guarantee that you would never be able to express this love?"

She stared at him blankly, and he chuckled again.

"Adelle." Reynard tried to rid himself of his smile. "Surely you are but a fawn. I have told him you were forced to go with me. That your actions were produced by my threats, but Jean believes our present friendship to be more. I have made it clear I think of you as a daughter, that our relationship was honorable, but he insists you love me as a woman loves a man."

Adelle listened quietly, her anger subsiding.

"If you wish this to change, if you wish his companionship as I think you do, then you need to make your affections clear." He took her father's knife from her belt and held it up.

"Chaboillier provided what he could for you. He gave you his wisdom. Think of the words he gave you when he feared he would not see you again. They were from his heart, and I add to them my own. Is not Jean Baptiste true and his loyalty lasting? He is a brave wiser than many, and his heart is strengthened daily by his faith.

"He can be an arrogant young buck when he chooses," he said with a hint of annoyance. "But his love for you is true, Adelle, and his devotion to me has never wavered. He carries the scars of Mighty Fox also; this I regret." Reynard placed the knife in her hand together with his pipe. "Red Earth would honor you. Chaboillier would not be disappointed. Hear the words of your fathers, one of flesh, both in spirit."

Adelle squeezed the knife and the pipe together tightly in her hand.

"Trust me in this," Reynard continued. "I will return, and you will have seen that this is so. It is not hate that you see. It is jealousy. Now I must tell you something more."

Adelle blinked at the change in his tone.

"I want to tell you what Chaboillier must have never told you." He paused, debating, perhaps, his next words.

Adelle frowned. "Just say it; please, Reynard."

"Your mother was a mètis. Not that anyone would guess, however. But Chaboillier kept it to himself, I think, so that his women would be respected by other Frenchmen."

Adelle was silent as she absorbed the news. It was like hearing gossip about a stranger. "She wasn't from Montreal?"

"Yes, I think that is where Chaboillier met her. She was an Iroquois' slave. She had been captured in a raid against the Wendat."

Adelle parted her lips in surprise. "How do you know all this?"

"He and my father were partners long before you were born. Sometimes we travelled together."

Adelle closed her eyes. A fraction of the blood coursing through her veins was Wendat? The real hoax had been on her all along.

"Adelle." Reynard touched her shoulder, and she opened her eyes.

"Was she of the turtle clan?" she asked barely above a whisper.

"I do not know," Reynard answered. "She was of the northern Wendat. Marie would know more."

It did not really matter anyway. The woman had always been a ghost and would probably remain so. "Thank you, Reynard, for everything, for being my friend and my protector."

He nodded and withdrew his hand from her shoulder. "I must go now. Remember what I said about Red Earth. "What you are searching for is in your hand, if you want it."

Adelle nodded her farewell as he turned to leave. She watched him pass through the gates and when she could see him no longer, she slipped her father's knife back into her belt and turned the pipe over in her hand. It was still warm from its use. Could Reynard be right about Jean? She wondered.

The sun was setting when Reynard reached Old Coyote's village. The dogs barked their familiar alarm, and children ran to tell their parents of his arrival. Reynard walked slowly into the village and was not surprised at the greeting that awaited him. The young men gathered solemnly, blocking his way. Big Hawk Flying led them. Reynard advanced until he stood before the warriors. He said nothing, waiting for them to speak first. He observed with a chilling realization that they carried their weapons. He pulled himself up bravely and held his chin high.

Dead Man's Honor

It was nearing twilight when the Jesuit returned to Pontchartrain. Adelle ran to meet him the moment he arrived.

"Father, have you come from the Huron village?" she asked.

He shook his head. "The Outawae," he answered. "Is something wrong?"

"It is Reynard," she answered walking beside him. "He has gone back to Old Coyote's village today."

"This is bad?" the Jesuit inquired.

Adelle considered his question. Father Francois, newly arrived, had much to learn of Wendat ways. He only knew what the Wendats wanted him to know. He, like she had been, was only acquainted with their culture from the outside, not the inside. Perhaps he would not understand the danger to Reynard. And danger may be the best word to describe it, she thought, for as the day had progressed the more she felt the impulse to pray for his safety.

"For him it is," she said finally.

"Then we must pray for him," the Jesuit said. "Trust in God, Adelle."

"Yes." She turned away, wandering absently out of the fort. Father Francois would pray; he was true to his promises. But she could not silence the thoughts turning over and over in her mind long enough to commit herself to prayer. She found herself on the high gray dirt road along the river and was surprised to see Jean approaching the fort.

"Salut," he called to her cheerfully. "It is a beautiful night, yes?" He did not wait for her answer. "I came to see Mighty Fox."

"He went to see Old Coyote– the Wendat village." She gestured. "He left early."

"Oh." He seemed disappointed.

She turned onto the path leading down to the river.

"Are you going somewhere?" he called after her.

She stopped. "No. Just walking. I was going to sit by the river and watch the night come."

"Oh," he said again.

She paused, looking back over her shoulder. For once he did not seem so sure of himself. "Want to come?" she said remembering what Reynard had told her.

He shrugged indifferently then smiled. "Yes."

Together they walked to the Teuchsagrondie River and sat on the rocks near the shoreline. The water was gray with shadows as the sun sank below the horizon behind them, and the first star appeared in the salmon pink sky.

Adelle could think of nothing to say. Her mind was full with worry over Reynard. The silence went on for some time, and she feared Jean was sorry he had come. He squatted next to the water, skimming stones across the current. She gave up on praying and went to stand near him.

"You are missing Reynard, yes?" he asked softly with his back to her.

Adelle twisted a long blade of grass around her finger. She walked to the water's edge and knelt beside him. "No," she answered quietly after considering it. "But I am worrying over him. I did not want him to go; it is true. But he would not have listened." She sighed.

"My father and his father were friends long ago. They are both dead. I do not wish for Reynard to die young. I wish no harm to come to him at all. His life has just begun, yes? But Chief Old Coyote was at Orontony's council, and he agreed to war. Reynard is Old Coyote's nephew, and Old Coyote raised him into Wendat manhood as his son. I did not tell the Jesuit all these things; he would not have understood."

Jean studied her intently.

"I fear that Old Coyote could hurt him far worse than Brave Arrow's revenge," she said. "Perhaps the wounds of his heart will make him suffer more harshly than anything his flesh has yet to endure. You know what might happen to him even more than I. I fear for him, Jean." She touched his arm and the warmth of his skin comforted her. "That is all."

Jean grasped her hand and pulled her up. "You forget, Adelle," he said. "He is not protected by any oki, or bag of herbs, or charms around his neck. His God is not a god of men, but of power, and He is able to keep him safe." Wisps of his long hair brushed his cheek as the evening breeze flowed in over the lake.

Her hand was safely enclosed in his. "You are right," she said at last. Thoughtfully, Adelle watched the white crested waves roll to shore and melt into a frothy foam on the sand. "He is not just Mighty Fox, son of Old Coyote, any more. He is a child of God, and he must walk the path God has given him." She squeezed Jean's hand, looking up into his kind brown eyes. "It is what is expected of us isn't it?"

"Yes," he answered. Jean held her arm gently and led the way back to the fort gate. The waves splashed to shore behind them as the moon rose, a huge orange orb on the lake's northeast horizon.

The braves stood in a menacing line not five feet from Reynard. Old Coyote pushed his way through them.

"Our friends in the white village told us that you live," he said. "Always like the fox, I say; he has escaped death. He has outwitted his hunter. And I watched for your coming. I knew you would come." Old Coyote spoke evenly as if he had measured his words many times, but his eyes did not mask the hurt Reynard had inflicted upon him.

Reynard had rehearsed his words also, but now as he faced Old Coyote, saw his pain, the man who was his father when he had none, his chosen words faded away. Reynard was left with nothing as he stood there, silent like a young boy. Tears blurred his vision.

Suddenly he remembered how he had left Red Earth standing wounded in the forest for choosing to be loyal to no man, only to that which was right. Betrayed, he had told him. Betrayed his friend and his people. Old Coyote would not understand but Reynard knew what he was feeling in some way. He had done what Jean had done: risked loyalty to either side in his effort to save lives, Wendat and French, friend and enemy. In truth it was the People's way as Jean had said. For if what Old Coyote had taught him was true, that the hurt of one is the hurt of all, then surely the well-being of one must be the well-being of all.

Reynard was humbled by his emotion and shamed before the warriors. He struggled to gain control of himself while Old Coyote remained a man of duty and Wendat wisdom, though the wrinkled skin on his sunken cheeks rippled with the clenching of his jaw. Deep within, beyond duty, Reynard sensed Old Coyote loved him as a son still. It is what Reynard needed to know.

"You must not come to the council fire," he told Reynard. "You will not sit with me and pass the pipe as Wendat. If you come again, it will be as the white comes, a white who has made enemies of his friends."

Reynard opened his mouth to speak and feared his emotion would overcome him. He looked into the eyes that had taught him to be a man, that had given love freely, but now refused his, that wished to sever every bond they had shared for thirty years.

Reynard knew if he desired to tell him anything it must be now, for he would never have the opportunity again. He wanted him to know why he acted against the tribe's wishes. He took a deep breath, desperately hoping for the words to speak. "You brought me to your fire," he began. "I was a young boy, taught by my white father to be white, and I grew. But I was not white. In your love, you taught me all things Wendat, and I prospered and grew to do many things for the People. But I am not Wendat.

"I am something I do not know. Does the panther have the jaws of the snake? Does the bear have the eye of the eagle? And yet, I am formed of two creatures, two worlds.

"The stream flows to the river, and the river to the lake. Then it is no longer a stream or a river but a lake. Its waters cannot be separated. Such is my spirit, Ayseta. Not only Wendat. Not only white. It is something larger, with cords bound to both people.

"This is wisdom given to me by the God of Light. Not the Wendat god, not the white god, but the Creator of both people. The Creator of the river, the stream and the lake Who made all things, and everything is under Him."

Old Coyote frowned. "You are a dreamer of dreams," he said. "Much oki has been given you. But you speak strange things."

"I turned from Orontondi," Reynard said, "not because I turned against The People, but because I turned from the English. We are only pawns in their hands."

"They offer us better trade," Old Coyote insisted. "I do not understand your concern. Your white tongue hinders your sight of the Wendat; this I know.

And you must be pushed away from my breast because of it. You must go now. No longer will we speak as father and son. I have no son named Mighty Fox."

Old Coyote turned away, his gray head held high. He walked into the cluster of braves, and the only sign of his sorrow was his clenched fists.

Reynard blinked away tears as Old Coyote disappeared behind the wall of men. "I am a man with two hearts," he whispered in Wendat. "One I leave on this sand, and I will never know it again." He stood for a minute, looking into the stern faces of the young men. He knew them all. Slowly he walked back to the river.

Three weeks passed with no news of Reynard. Jean had traded with a Wendat party to the north of Pontchartrain, but they were of a different village he said and were not familiar with Old Coyote. It was possible they spoke the truth, Adelle thought. Not all Wendat tribes went to Orontony's council. Many were from Huronia across the lake like her mother. Old Coyote had ties to Orontony because they had been settled near Pontchartrain during the same time.

"No news is a good sign," Jean assured Adelle as he plunked a bag of flour on the Jesuit's table.

"Thank you, Monsieur Baptiste. I appreciate your care concerning my food supply." Father Francois took the bag and emptied it into a crock.

Adelle turned to watch him.

"That was the flour crock, yes?" he asked.

"It will do I suppose." She returned to the preparations for his meal. "How could it be good news?" she asked Jean, chopping herbs with vigor. "He should have returned by now." She tossed the pile into a pot and swiped the knife on her sleeve.

"It means he survived his visit with Old Coyote." Jean glanced at the Jesuit.

"How do you know that?" She regarded them both. "Am I the only one concerned for him?"

"I know because his death, or torture, would be published as a warning to others ever contemplating going against the tribe like he did."

She sheathed her knife.

"No news indicates two possibilities," he continued. "One, they wanted to kill him but feared the fort's retaliation for the murder of a Frenchman. Two, Old Coyote has given him a pardon of some type. Hopefully it satisfies the braves' desire to punish Reynard for defying the tribe's vote to join Orontony."

"Hopefully?"

Jean shrugged.

"I didn't realize how serious his circumstances were." The Jesuit sat down on his bench.

"But," Jean said, "since it was probably known that DeLongueuil wouldn't have lifted a finger to bring Reynard's killer to justice—"

"Thank you for reminding us." Adelle stooped to put wood on the small fire under the pot.

"Old Coyote must have shown mercy and spared him somehow," Jean finished.

"Wonderful! That is good news, Adelle. See?"

Adelle glanced at the priest and pulled another pot from under the coals at the side of the fire.

"There is more news if you care to hear it."

"About Reynard?" Adelle asked.

"About Orontony," Jean answered.

She sliced the venison roast in the pan. "Please tell it."

"Orontony has gotten himself in real trouble with the forts since last June. Not many Wendats remain loyal to him now, at least in the presence of the commandant. It is rumored he wants peace with the French. This is what my Odawa friends are saying."

"Peace!" the Jesuit cried. "He certainly changed convictions quickly."

Adelle fished the boiled vegetables from the pot and arranged them alongside the meat on Father Francois' plate.

"Hah," Jean scoffed. "It is only to save himself from punishment for the five murders committed in his village. He is not sincere. But a Wendat is never sincere even when times are good."

Adelle replayed the words in her head as she slid the plate in front of Father Francois. "Never?" she asked.

"Well, rarely."

"I am Wendat," Adelle announced.

The priest cleared his throat. "I think I will enjoy my supper in the autumn air." He picked up his plate. "Excuse me," he said with a nod to Jean.

"You probably think that proves your point," she said to Jean ignoring the Jesuit. "That I am not sincere, yes?"

"I'm sorry—"

"No, do not apologize for your convictions. You wouldn't want to be accused of saying something insincere certainly."

Jean stared at her.

"You are not sorry anyway are you?" Adelle was amazed at the truth.

Jean shrugged again. "Our tribes have not been on the best of terms—"

"What does that have to do with anything?"

"Because they have been fickle friends!" Jean finished.

"Is this why you do not care if Reynard is tortured and never returns?"

"I never said that. You are exaggerating."

"Ah-huh! Exaggerating? You mean lying? No you have never said it outright. Are all Odawa deceitful? Pretending to be friends but they are really spies?" She grabbed a piece of meat and put the lids on both pots.

"All right," Jean admitted. "I am sorry."

"No it is not all right. I am fond of Reynard. I hoped you were too. But he and I are Wendat. People you seem to disdain."

Jean held up his hand. "I understand your anger."

"No. You do not. And I am not angry." She was annoyed.

Jean opened his mouth and shut it. "I am going to leave now."

"No." she said firmly. "I am leaving." She brushed past him out the door.

Father Francois smiled from his perch on the stool by the garden. "Supper was very good!" he called to her.

"Of course it was," she muttered and bit into the piece of meat she carried.

Later, the news about Orontony went rippling through the Indian villages and traders' routes. The latest was that Orontony was coming to Pontchartrain to re-establish his loyalty to the French and had agreed to dissolve his friendship with the British traders. This information posed no threat to her, Adelle thought. But for Reynard, Orontony's presence near the fort could be another matter. Perhaps his absence was providential.

Adelle leaned closer to the firelight to thread her needle. She was intent on making a dress for herself like the French habitant women wore from the cloth Jean had left for her at the priest's house. She hadn't talked to him since they had argued, but DeLongueuil was meeting with tribes and Jean was kept busy in his service. Suddenly the cabin door opened and shut with a bang.

"Heathens!" The Jesuit tossed his large black hat on the table and tore open his long coat.

Adelle laid the sewing aside and filled his bowl. It was a rare sight for Father Francois to show his anger.

"Drunken heathens! It is no wonder these Indians regard me with contempt!" he bellowed.

She closed the door quietly behind her as she left, and the cool night air was full with the sound of merry traders, singing, howling and dancing for whatever reason they could think of. Usually their celebrations ended in someone getting into a fight, and they would brawl until their drunkenness overtook them or they forgot what they were fighting about. Their Indian friends were welcome to join in, of course. This is what had rankled the Jesuit. All his efforts to build the church and save souls were in vain upon the arrival of the traders.

The habitants were indifferent to the goings on, however, and as long as no one bothered them, they attended church, tended their crops and livestock, wishing for nothing more. Truly, Adelle thought as she walked to her little house, it was not a bad way to view life.

"Adelle!"

She paused outside her door. Jean stood in the street.

"I am on my way to the commandant's. You want to accompany me?"

"I do not know."

"Are you starting again?"

"I mean is it an official visit?"

"It is the commandant, Adelle. Yes. It will not take long though."

"But the goings on." It was not always safe to be out in it.

"We can watch."

"Wait, all right?" She placed her sewing inside and joined him. "Thank you for the material. I am making a new dress. At least I hope so."

Jean chuckled. "You accept my apology then?"

Adelle sighed. "I guess so. But what does it mean to our friendship if you are not on good terms with the Wendat?"

"Nothing. Do you know why I came to the fort that day to help Reynard? To help you?"

Adelle looked up at him. "No."

"Because I respect Reynard, and I wanted you both to be happy."

"Oh."

"Does that settle your doubts about me?"

Adelle grinned. "Yes."

"Good. Wait for me here." He indicated the commandant's stoop. "I will be one moment."

Adelle sat down calmly watching the ruckus, and true to his word Jean came out and sat beside her. He smiled as a short stout man sent a spindly young trader sprawling on the ground. Two women set upon the fallen man at once, going through his pockets then bickering over the contents.

Adelle giggled. "The man on the ground is Nicolas le Sueur. Papa said he never could hold his brandy."

"Apparently not," Jean remarked. "The other is Jacques Buchard. He would wrestle a bear if he went too long without a fight."

"Reynard was right, you know." She rested her elbow on her knee and leaned her chin in her hand. "He said we French were fools to believe we could change the People. To Christianity I mean. Look," she said with a nod toward the traders. "We need to change ourselves first. It is not Father Francois' fault."

Jean pondered this and looked again to the cheerful mob of traders and their employees. "Is he vexed again?" Jean chuckled. "Wait until you see him in the spring. Broad is the way that leads to destruction and many there be which go in," he quoted.

"But narrow is the way that leads to life," Adelle finished. "I am glad you walk the narrow way," she said, smiling.

He reached for her hand and touched it to his cheek. "I am glad we both walk the same way."

His eyes were soft and warm toward her as when she first met him. She wanted him to look upon her like that forever.

"I wish to always walk our pathway together," he said.

Her heart filled at his words. "Then our wish is the same," she answered quietly.

He closed his eyes and pressed her hand to his lips, the sweet warmth of his breath caressing her hand.

"I have prayed it would be so," he whispered. He drew her close in his embrace and kissed her, his love no longer a fearful hope.

Reynard travelled with no destination in mind. Far into the heart of the land and back to Okswego he went. The news about Orontondi had found him by gossiping traders. But Reynard discovered his true comfort in what he loved best: seeing each new bend in the river, experiencing each new day as a challenge to be won. So it was here, next to the lake that he settled for a time alone, consoled by good fishing and the gift of each sunrise.

Reynard established himself high up off the bank with a good view of the water and the forest at his back to block the prevailing wind. For many days this spot was his home. The sun was losing its warmth as the days passed, and the daylight was growing shorter, bit by bit, fading leaf by fading leaf.

So too his sorrow concerning Old Coyote lessened, bit by bit. It was a wound just beginning to heal. But he could not live like a spirit haunted by the past anymore. The time had come to face his loss and gain strength from it.

This included confronting Brave Arrow, he decided. If he were to live the rest of his life in peace, these things had to be settled. He could not bear it if his life as Mighty Fox would be forever scorned among the People. He did not deceive himself, however. He had been the first among the braves to kill for honor, to gather in the worship of spirits and to fully embrace the sinful way of love. Now even though he had grown to be a man of dignity and great honor, his achievements shamed him.

But the memory of Mighty Fox, as evil as any French might regard him, must not be blotted out in the People's mind because of the one last act he had attempted. For this act, above any other, he should be remembered. He had come to believe his life held more importance to the Wendat than any feat of bravery he had ever accomplished. For he was living proof of a God who loved him and had chosen him to bring honor upon Himself by keeping him alive.

One morning it was like dropping a stone into his heart, so great was this assurance. He paddled the rest of the day, his mind set on this one thought. By nightfall he reached the bay. He rounded the shore, soon pulling his canoe onto the yellow sandy beach not far from the place he had arrived with Adelle almost a year ago. He calmly walked the well worn path to the village. No one expected him here, unlike his home village so near Pontchartrain which was informed of the comings and goings there.

As he neared the walls, he prepared his heart as Old Coyote had taught him, for this advice was still valid. "God," he whispered. "You are my Father, but I am not worthy to be called a son. A child should know his father's voice, but I cannot hear if there is darkness between us. If I act only to restore my pride, then my purpose is without honor. Take the offerings in my heart and make them pleasing to You."

He entered the village and cried out his familiar greeting in Wendat. The People stared as a dog approached him wagging its tail. More people came from their lodges, and children scurried to their parents. The People watched him, puzzled by the dog's acceptance of a stranger.

"Do not be afraid!" Reynard assured them. He realized he possessed little of the appearance of Mighty Fox the warrior, but perhaps this was in his favor.

The familiar voice booming from an unfamiliar form terrified them, and braves gathered to defend the People as Reynard continued on his way to the center of their village.

Brave Arrow was standing across from him now, his expression showing only careful scrutiny, awaiting what was to come next. Perhaps he was perplexed at the arrival of what he deemed a naive Frenchman, or at least an uninformed one.

Reynard opened his shirt. "Look upon me, Brave Arrow."

Brave Arrow's eyes were wide as he stared at the hideous scars then upward to Reynard's face.

"I am Mighty Fox!" Reynard roared and Brave Arrow's courage seemed to visibly fade away. "My People, I looked, and I saw what would happen to you." Reynard spread his arms wide. "Your great chief has been humbled because his way is not pure. He is like a dog who comes to his master with his tail between his legs. You are knocked down by the breath of the whites. Someday he will be broken by them. The honored feathers of Orontondi will be carried by the wind and trampled by all those who come after him.

"I did not want this to be so. I have only love for you. Brave Arrow's hatred has not destroyed me. My blood is made new by the Living God. He is the only God, and I am safe in Him."

Reynard crossed the open space between him and Brave Arrow. He felt no more hatred for him. "No arrow can take away my victory, my honor," Reynard said. "I am Mighty Fox, your friend."

Reynard reached to touch Brave Arrow's shoulder, but the warrior stiffened and closed his eyes as if preparing to be struck dead. A little girl began to cry, but her mother smothered the sound with her hand. They were all afraid of him. Their fear blinded them, he thought in dismay. He was defeated in a battle for truth that did not seem possible to win anymore. He stood searching the crowd. Running Dog stood next to Shining Water, a baby cradled in her arms. Strangely enough there was no fear in his eyes. But in this he was alone. Slowly Reynard turned away and without a sound walked out of the village, the dog following him for some distance.

He retrieved his canoe, and was halfway back to the tip of the bay when he pulled to shore at one of his favorite fishing spots. He sat a long time drinking in the beauty around him. The moon kept watch like a glowing white crescent against the blackened sky. The waves rippled to shore reflecting a glitter of moonlight here and there across the ebony expanse of water which stretched as far as he could see. Stars gleamed from their perches far away in the inky depths of heaven.

He felt discouraged. It was as if his words had met empty air, like they had fallen to the ground, and yet, he felt a task had been completed. With dawning expectation he studied the point far on the horizon where water met sky and wondered where his faith would direct him next. Suddenly a strange rustling sound jolted him into the present. It was faint and fleeting, but it did not follow the rhythm of the waves spilling onto shore. It had come from behind, from the trees. Someone or something was near. Reynard inhaled. He did not smell the familiar thick scent of a bear. Perhaps Brave Arrow had gathered his courage and had come to regain his honor. Perhaps it was a group of braves that sought him out.

Reynard stood and felt for his knife tucked readily in its sheath at his waist, but its handle felt cold and peculiar in his hand. Amazed, he realized he no longer had the eiachia of a brave. He did not have the emotion necessary to kill an enemy. Slowly he sat back down. He stared across the water, but his trained eye observed any motion on either side of him. He sat seemingly unaware of anything amiss, and yet fully alert. He was not startled then when he heard footsteps behind him, soft as leather brushing leather in the sand. He turned and rose to his feet, prepared for whatever fate awaited him.

It was Running Dog. He was alone, Reynard observed, and his leggings were wet from the knee down. He had probably followed him to the bay and watched in which direction he paddled. Then he had kept pace with him on foot through the trees.

"Ha-en-ye-ha," Reynard greeted him, but Running Dog said nothing and kept his distance. It did not seem he desired to come any closer.

"Do not be afraid, brother. It is I, Mighty Fox, not a spirit that you see," Reynard reassured him.

Running Dog crossed his arms over his chest. "I hear the voice of Mighty Fox," he said. "I see the flesh of a man that is only a shadow of him."

Reynard chuckled. "Brave Arrow is a good warrior; his aim is true. This flesh has travelled to the edge of death, and the path back into life was full of sharp rocks. Come." Reynard motioned. "Sit with me as my brother."

Running Dog hesitated, but he crossed the stretch of beach between them and folded himself down onto the damp sand beside Reynard. He still seemed wary of him.

"Why did you come?" Reynard asked.

"I wanted to know if your words were true," he answered.

"And what is it that you believe now that you are here?" Reynard pressed him.

Running Dog traced the designs on the side of his moccasin with his finger. "I was with Brave Arrow that day," he said quietly.

Reynard straightened. He hadn't considered that Running Dog would be among the war party. Hastily he replayed the images in his mind, but he could not remember seeing his friend. Running Dog avoided his gaze.

"I saw his arrows pierce your skin and sink deep into your flesh," he continued. "A coldness swept over me like I have never known. I did not understand. It was as if you were pierced, but it was my blood that seeped into the water. I watched the river carry you past my canoe, but when I turned again to look, I saw only the river."

He swept his hand outward toward the lake. "I saw only water. Mighty Fox was gone, and I knew the spirits had hidden you. In my heart I believed Brave Arrow had not the power to kill you. In my heart I knew Mighty Fox did not die that day. I have thought long on all these things. Now I hear your words, and I know it is your voice. I have thought long concerning your actions, but now I sit again next to my brother, and there are no questions which demand an answer. You have come, you have spoken, and it is enough."

Reynard was quiet. Surely, he did not have a more faithful friend among the Wendat. Perhaps Running Dog was the only man he knew who could see into his heart.

"What are the words the People speak?" he asked at last.

"Flies-Strong-Against-The-Wind believes that your spirit lives in a white man now," Running Dog answered. "And that you have chased the animals away from our hunting grounds in revenge. They are discussing what must be done to make peace with you." He smiled. "Brave Arrow has begun a fast to protect him from the evil spirit he thinks visited him."

"I seek revenge on no one," Reynard said ignoring Running Dog's amusement with Brave Arrow. "I will ask the Black Robes' God to bring you food, to clothe you for the winter. If it is done as I ask, then you will know the power He has. Then you will know it is to Him that you must give honor."

Reynard so wanted him to understand. "Orontondi has been defeated, do you see this?" he asked. "Can you see the British soldiers did not stand with him to help him? I do not know what will happen now for the People," Reynard said, shaking his head sadly. "But I believe it will come, and we will not be able to change it."

Running Dog listened intently.

"It is like the power of the sun as it rises, or the lake when it begins to roll," Reynard explained. "It is a force that cannot be stopped. So it is with the coming of the whites. There is no arrow strong enough to stop them. There are not enough arrows to stop them. It began before we were given life, and it will continue after we are dead. Orontondi is eager for a war he will not win. The Wendat will suffer no matter which path they choose, but there is no honor for any man who dies foolishly. Hear the words of your friend."

A thin slice of red began to appear on the horizon as the day began to break. The two men sat in reflective silence as the morning's radiance grew, each knowing the other's reluctance to end the time together. Finally Running Dog stood and waited for Reynard to do the same.

"I will always hold your words," Running Dog said. "I respect their wisdom because I know the heart that speaks them. But my place is here, to make a home for Shining Water and my son. I will do what I need to do to make them happy, to keep them safe, to live as Wendat."

Reynard looked upon Running Dog with a new respect. He had grown the heart of a true warrior. Despite the People's fear of him, Reynard's pride and love for them were strong, and for Running Dog he desired God's favor.

"You are honest and loyal," he said. "I will always remember you as my friend. I will pray all things best for you and your family. Your son will be proud of you. He will hold his head high and walk steadily behind you. Others will follow him, and you will be satisfied."

Reynard reached into his pocket. "I give this to you." He held out his braided scalplock, the eagle feathers and red cloth still attached. "Remember my spirit, my love for my People. Let it be a charm if you wish, a gift to your son."

"I will tell him of Mighty Fox, great warrior of the Wendat, a seer for his People and my friend forever." Running Dog held the gift tightly and touched it to his heart.

Reynard embraced Running Dog heartily to seal their act of loyalty to each other, and Running Dog returned this display of affection.

"Ha-en-ye-ha," Running Dog said.

"Scan-o-nie-ha-en-ye-ha," Reynard answered, and Running Dog turned and walked back into the forest. Reynard stood alone on the sandy shore as the orange sun crested the horizon and transformed the sky into a flaming sweep of pink and violet. He grabbed his canoe with one hand, shoving it into the shallows. The water was cold as he splashed through the water and stepped into the canoe. He paddled swiftly to the mouth of the bay and turned north.

Adelle would be waiting for him, he thought, and a tender warmth filled him. He glanced back over his shoulder as he rounded the forested peninsula, watching the smoke from the village cooking fires curl into the early morning sky far away. He smiled faintly, bittersweet memories tugging on his heart as he left forever his friends and this country Saundustee.

Journey's End

Orontony's arrival in Pontchartrain was not without its pomp. The French for their part desired to make a show of authority, discreetly of course, with their nobly clad militia an ever present reminder of their believed superiority. The Wendat, on the other hand, out of necessity, kept their military status low-key in order to appease the French; this was their intent. One couldn't help notice, however, the arrogant swagger of the braves as they made their way to DeLongueuil, Adelle thought. The commandant, no matter how hard he tried, could not distinguish their pride in being Wendat.

Orontony had mustered all the humility he could manage to stand before DeLongueuil with an apology on his lips, Adelle marveled. No longer were his words spiteful daggers of hate. They were honey-sweet flowers of friendship.

"I think the saints have penetrated his conscience," Father Francois declared as he and Adelle watched the goings on with the rest of the habitants.

Adelle raised her eyebrows. "They had a hide of iron to chip away at. I am not sure they've reached his flesh yet."

"Not so, Adelle!" the Jesuit cried. "I have met Chief Nicholas myself, and I find him a very amicable man."

"Amicable before his accusers," Adelle argued.

"Those are harsh words to hurl upon a Christian. I would not be so hasty with your judgment of him," he advised. "You may risk bringing judgment upon yourself." Clearly the Jesuit was becoming annoyed with her opinions.

"Father Francois, I mean you no disrespect," she began, "but the only reason most of these Indians are baptized is because the French pay them more money for their trade goods if they do so. Baptizing them and giving them a Christian name does not mean they are Christians."

At this the Jesuit's face flushed a deep red. "Then what would you have us do?"

Adelle did not mean to offend him, but the Wendat people were no longer a distant culture to her. They were her friends, people who had accepted her as family, and she did not like to see them used by men French, British, or Indian.

"Well, they should not be bribed for one thing," Adelle answered. "But Chief Nicholas is a man who uses opportunity to better himself. I would not fling my trust before him so readily. What happened to those French traders was not anything a Christian should condone, and yet he desired it. I do not believe he could change so quickly. I am afraid it is not repentance that you see but cunning diplomacy.

"If you would have seen him in his own village, among his own people as I have," Adelle went on, "you would agree. For some, it is not enough to take their word. We need to understand how they think first. If you were in his place what would you do?"

The Jesuit positioned his wide-brimmed black hat on his head. "Perhaps you are right. You have more experience in these things than I have. But I must remain in love toward this man, choosing to think the best of him. If his actions prove otherwise, then I have done nothing wrong; I have not placed a stumbling block before him."

Adelle understood the rebuke in his words, but she was not angry. He was right. But there was also a time for being as wise as serpents. The Jesuit took his leave, and Adelle made her way through the crowd as some Wendats from Old Coyote's village arrived with others straggling in behind them. Marie was not one of them, Adelle observed, but she was not surprised.

Tonight the celebration would begin, the Dance of the Calumet. It was said that performing the dance was a symbol of the compromise of peace between the two nations. She sat on the edge of the common as the drums began, and Jean soon joined her.

The Wendat dancers lined up as the drums beat. "Ni, Ha, Ni, Ni, Na, Ha, Ni," the singers began.

"It is a beautiful dance to witness, yes?" Jean spoke quietly.

"I have witnessed many good things from these people," Adelle answered.

"I only wish," he said, "that Orontony truly desired peace. He is too proud to lead his people into submission before the French. It is not his way. "

"I have said the very same to Father Francois."

"The French have their deficiencies, but I am beginning to understand the People are better off maintaining an alliance with them. My friend, Obwandiyag, agrees."

Adelle jostled him. "Don't you wish Reynard could see Orontony now? I wish he knew Reynard was alive. The old–" But she held her tongue. Perhaps the Jesuit was right. She did not show enough love to her enemy. But even love is not without discipline, she thought.

Jean smiled at her. "This is a game, Adelle. Played between scheming men. Reynard would see Orontony and know his meekness is for a time. DeLongueuil won this time; Orontony plays the loser. The funny thing is, both sides play by different rules." His voice faded into the din of rising voices.

Jean leaned close to her. "We still have much to be thankful for because of Orontony." He smiled, covering her hand with his.

She grinned, warmed by the tender light his eyes held for her.

The trees were bare sketches against the pale gray sky when Reynard returned to the fort. He dropped his canoe on the browning grass and confidently approached the Jesuit's house. He rapped heartily on the door, and Father Francois opened it wide.

"Reynard!"

"Bonjour," Reynard greeted him.

"Come in," the Jesuit invited and stepped aside. "Look, I am drying fish!"

Reynard raised his eyebrows. Indeed, he thought. A rack of fish stood next to the fireplace. He didn't have the heart to tell the kind priest the fish would dry better where the smoke would flavor it. That was the point, after all.

"You are looking for Adelle, yes?" Father Francois continued. He smiled slyly. "Well, there are certain goings on since last I have seen you. I performed the highest of blessing upon them a while ago, yes?"

Reynard grinned at the man's good humor. "It is good," he said.

"I agree, my friend. I agree. Now Jean's farm is the last along the habitant's road." He pointed north. "Just before the Outawae village."

"Merci," Reynard said, handing him a leather pouch filled with pemmican. He had a feeling the Jesuit would be needing it.

"Au revoir!" Father Francois called after him as he turned to go. "Au revoir!"

And Reynard left the fort the same way he had come, by canoe. The road stretched north and south along the river and was packed hard by frequent travel to and from the fort. But Reynard returned to the river because travelling the water was faster. He drifted along the shore slowly, the habitants' farms above him on the hill and sprawled on either side of the road in some spots.

He gazed up at the high bank, observing with a curious eye the smattering of log buildings: house, barn and lean-to. The houses were small, but the barns were almost three times bigger. Both had steeply pitched roofs where below pigs squealed, and a rooster crowed. A man whose scraggly beard only covered his jaws and chin was carrying an armload of wood into his house. A funny, cone-shaped hat of red and green with a string hanging from its tip adorned his head. He was followed by his son carrying another load of wood that was half hidden by the wolf coat thrown over the boy's shoulders.

It was strange to think of, Reynard thought when he had passed the small house, this settling in just one place forever. The land around the lakes was far too large to limit oneself to a narrow plot of earth. Finally the last house loomed ahead. Reynard guessed this must be Jean's. It looked much the same as the others, though he saw no animals routing around its yard.

"Salut!" he called, pulling in at a crude dock.

Adelle and Jean rounded the corner of the house, their arms full of just picked squash. Adelle nearly dropped hers when she saw Reynard.

"Reynard!" she cried, smiling broadly. "I was hoping you were coming soon."

Jean dumped the squash next to the doorway and crossed the yard to greet him. "It is good to see you," he said, reaching out his hand to grasp Reynard's shoulder.

Reynard accepted the warm greeting with pleasure and reciprocated in equal fashion. Turning to Adelle, he smiled playfully. "What is this I find? So worried I would not return, and I am the one who must come looking for you!"

Adelle blushed and lowered her eyes quickly. “Come,” she said. “Rest and tell us where you have been.” She pointed to a sunny spot near the river.

Reynard accepted her invitation and sat on the ground.

“I will get some cider,” Jean said and left them alone.

Reynard looked back at the little farm, and Adelle couldn’t help noticing the disdainful expression with which he beheld it.

“So is this where your journey ends, Adelle? Is this what you had hoped for when you left Chaboillier?”

His tone was almost pitying, Adelle thought. She followed his gaze. The tiny house sat peacefully along the river, a wisp of gray smoke curling upward from its chimney into the bright blue sky dotted with frothy piles of white clouds. She smiled slowly, a great peace welling in her heart.

“Yes,” she said turning to him again. “I believe the Lord has brought Jean and me together as you said. It is a different life than I have known, I admit. But I am ready to settle, Reynard. My whole life has been travelling, like a voyageur sometimes. It was Papa’s life, but now is my season with Jean.”

Reynard nodded. “It is good then,” he agreed. “My season as Mighty Fox has passed also.” He gazed across the water. “I am no longer welcome in the Wendat village.”

Adelle frowned. She realized what this meant between him and Old Coyote.

“I will endure,” he said simply and shrugged his shoulders.

But Adelle could sense the tender wound beneath his indifference. “I am sorry,” she said. “Perhaps it will change in time? Chief Orontony is no longer followed. You said the French would hold his feathers and they do.”

Jean returned and poured two mugs of cider. He held one out to Reynard and smiled. “My father used to make it,” he said of the cider. “I have tried.” He shrugged and gave the other mug to Adelle.

"It is good– this cider?" Reynard asked. He smelled the contents and looked up, waiting for an answer before he drank.

Jean smiled. "It is not your French brandy."

Reynard sipped the tart liquid and scowled at first, but tipped the mug again. Presently he handed the empty mug to Jean. "I am leaving for Missilimakinak," he said. He turned to Adelle. "Your father was wise and his words have guided me also. I believe I will find healing when I revisit the beginning. I believe your God will strengthen me to do this."

Adelle leaned forward. "He will," she assured him. "He has given me strength when I had none left. And He has given me hope when there was no reason for it." For once she did not fear his going. She understood what Marie had told her, that this was his way. After all, Papa had been molded from the same clay had he not?

"He is your God also, Mighty Fox," Jean said. "He is the ancient sustenance of life, of our spirit, just as corn sustains our body. He is our Provider and our Savior. We are more than friends because of Him." Jean thumped his heart with his fist. "We are family," he said. "When you go, Father, I will wait for your return. In my mouth will be your name, and on the wind, the smell of your pipe."

Reynard grasped Jean's shoulder, and Jean returned the embrace. Reynard's eyes glistened, and Adelle realized the respect Jean had given him, respect that his own people refused him.

"I am honored," was all Reynard said, but it was obvious he was greatly moved by Jean's words.

Adelle was quiet for some time. A trio of ducks splashed noisily on the sparkling water, and their chatter echoed along the bank. Surely things had changed since that fateful day last autumn, she thought. God had worked all things for her good.

Jean talked to Reynard in the things of conversations of men, of trapping and fishing and the state of their canoes. Jean filled their cups again. Did he know how much she loved him? She wondered. Did he know the extent she admired his courage and loyalty and tenderness? Only God knew the riches of her thoughts. He knew how to provide for her. He knew what was best for her, and it was He who gave her this love as a blessing forever.

Papa would be pleased. She glanced proudly at Jean and with a dawning realization understood Shining Water's loyal admiration for Running Dog. She turned to Reynard. He still wore Wendat leggings and moccasins, and though his hair was like any Frenchman's, his face was cleanly shaved. He would never be truly French, nor truly Wendat, Adelle thought. As much as Jean refused to be cast into one mold, so Reynard would stand apart, learning to walk with God the path chosen for him alone.

And surely each was responsible for their own journey on this path, Adelle thought. She was glad to be chosen, glad to have obeyed and thankful to be loved by a Heavenly Father. For with this love she had been given, she had been taught to love more deeply. God had provided for her through Reynard, his wisdom, his protection and his love. Through her, God had supplied Reynard with a genuine love filled with truth.

"I must go," Reynard was saying.

She rose and walked to the river's edge beside Reynard. "I will miss you," she said as he stooped to grasp the gunwale of his canoe. She couldn't hide the catch in her voice.

"I will come again," he said. "To trade in Pontchartrain, to visit..." He touched her shoulder. "I will miss you too, Little Turtle."

He slid the canoe into the water.

"Wait!" Adelle cried, splashing into the shallow water. She hugged him goodbye. "Yu-now-moi-eh." I love you, she whispered in his ear.

He brushed the side of her cheek with his rough hand and smiled. "I will come in the spring. I still owe you beaver pelts from last fall, remember? I made an agreement with Chaboillier." He deftly crawled into his vessel.

Adelle smiled. "In the spring then."

"Always in the spring," he said to them both and pushed off with the tip of his paddle. He smiled over his shoulder.

Adelle walked back up the bank, and Jean held her close as they waved goodbye. Together they watched him paddle slowly upriver, and they stood silently on the bank long after he had disappeared from sight. A flock of black-headed geese passed overhead, sweeping low over the silver river, the whisper of their wings the only sound.

Epilogue

The true account concerning the Conspiracy of Chief Nicholas may be found in these books: *Pontiac and the Indian Uprising* by Howard H. Peckham, pages 30-33; *The City of Detroit* by Clarence Burton; *Michigan A History of the Wolverine State* by Willis F. Dunbar.

Odawa language translations are taken from Anishinaabemowin on the Web and http://www. Anishinaabemdaa.com.

Wendat translations are taken from *Vocabularies of the Shawanese and Wyandott Languages, Etc* by Indian agent John Johnston.

Unfortunately, the Wendat language is a language in peril today. The last people to speak fluent Huron died in the 1960s— truly a monumental death since language is the spoken expression of the spirit of a people.

If you would like to donate to the ongoing effort of language study for future generations, please contact your local tribal government. To donate specifically to the Wendat or to buy Wendat language materials, check out these websites: Wyandotte Nation of Oklahoma and Native Languages of the Americas.

D. F

www.ingramcontent.com/pod-product-compliance
Lightning Source LLC
Chambersburg PA
CBHW060625310726
48982CB00003B/679

* 9 7 8 0 9 7 6 6 2 6 8 1 7 *